Oranges for the Son of Alexander Levy

Isabelle
A Story in Shots

Praise for *Oranges for the Son of Alexander Levy*

'Nella Bielski writes out of the experience of obstruction, exile and betrayal (both personal and political), but the tone is hopeful and humane' – Hermione Lee, *Observer*

'Her delicate sense of humour runs like an electric beam illuminating the sombre landscape . . . Mme Bielski writes beautifully' – Selina Hastings, *Daily Telegraph*

'A rare combination of affection for everything, of acceptance and intelligence' – Hilary Bailey, *Guardian*

Praise for *Isabelle: A Story in Shots*

'A tantilizing enigma, Berger and Bielski's filmic approach is appropriate to Isabelle Eberhardt's literally dramatic life, and the symmetry of the imagery is an indication of the artistry of this work' – *Observer*

'A crisp, intriguing portrait of an extraordinarily enigmatic and interesting woman' — *Kirkus Reviews*

'Deft, almost Chekhovian . . . The lovely economy of their writing lends this new character a vitality allied to, but separate from, that of the original Isabelle'
– Ruth Pavey, *Hampstead & Highgate Express*

'Possesses both beauty and insight, illuminating once again the life of one of the most fascinating of late nineteenth century women' – Peter Burton, *Gay Times*

Oranges for the Son of Alexander Levy

Nella Bielski

translated by John Berger and Lisa Appignanesi

Isabelle

A Story in Shots

John Berger and Nella Bielski

ARCADIA BOOKS
LONDON

Arcadia Books Limited
15–16 Nassau Street
London W1W 7AB

Oranges for the Son of Alexander Levy
This edition published by Arcadia Books 2001
First published in the United Kingdom by Writers and Readers Publishing
Cooperative 1982
Originally published in French by Mercure de France 1979
Copyright © Nella Bielski 1979
English translation copyright © John Berger and Lisa Appignanesi 1982

Isabelle: A Story in Shots
This edition published by Arcadia Books 2001
First published by Arcadia Books 1998
Copyright © Nella Bielski and John Berger 1998

A catalogue record for this book is available from the British Library

ISBN 1–900850–33–8

Printed and bound in the United Kingdom by Bell & Bain Ltd., Glasgow

Arcadia Books distributors are as follows:
in the UK and elsewhere in Europe:
Turnaround Publishers Services
Unit 3, Olympia Trading Estate
Coburg Road
London N22 6TZ

in the USA and Canada:
Consortium Book Sales and Distribution, Inc.
1045 Westgate Drive
St Paul, MN 55114—1065

in Australia:
Tower Books
PO Box 213
Brookvale, NSW 2100

in New Zealand:
Addenda
Box 78224
Grey Lynn
Auckland

in South Africa:
Peter Hyde Associates (Pty) Ltd
PO Box 2856
Cape Town 8000

This edition is dedicated with love and respect to the memory of
Glenn Thompson

About the Authors

Nella Bielski was born in Russia just before World War II. She is part of that generation who were evacuated to the Urals during the German attack and had just reached adolescence when Stalin died. She was one of the few women to study at the Moscow Philosophy Faculty.

Bielski's prize-winning fiction includes *After Arkadia* (Viking). Together with John Berger, she has written two plays, *A Question of Geography* and *Goya's Last Portrait*, as well as *Isabelle: A Story in Shots*. She lives in Paris.

John Berger won the Booker Prize in 1972 with his novel *G*. His celebrated fiction includes *Pig Earth*, *To the Wedding* and *King*. His non-fiction includes *Ways of Seeing*, *Another Way of Telling* and, most recently, *The Shape of a Pocket*.

About the Co-translator:

Lisa Appignanesi's latest books include *Sanctuary* (Bantam) and *Losing the Dead* (Vintage).

Oranges for the Son of Alexander Levy

Nella Bielski

translated by John Berger and Lisa Appignanesi

To My Mother

I no longer knew where I was with Paul. He was living, without pretending otherwise, with another woman. Mother Xenia was dying. The night before I had mashed a banana with some cream cheese for her. She was lying back against her pillow. Everything tired her these days, lying, sitting, eating, not eating. Twice a day they gave her injections. I don't know of what. Something which helped her to keep going.

She kept going. For the last three years, that's what I had done too. First I kept going for days, then for months, then through the seasons. Let's stop there with the seasons. I kept going, that's all. The previous autumn had not been so bad. That's when I had the courage to throw Paul out. There was no longer any reason for not finishing with the whole affair. But this only accounted for one autumn.

Mother was dying. It was winter, February, and Mother was going to be dead by the fourth of March. I was going to hear the news in Gif sur Yvette in the Ile de France. Now I

1

was in Moscow for ten days. I slept at the Hotel Metropole or at the house of some friends in Herzen Street. Each morning I took a taxi to Zelenograd, the green belt city, forty kilometres away. Mother had rented a new flat there to die in. I had never seen this flat before. It was not home. Of my home all that was left were my mother and Aunt Tanya— Aunt Tanya who has been good during all the seventy years of her life and who comes from the Ukraine. It was she who announced to Mother that her third new-born child had sexual parts in the shape of a half-moon. So, in a way, it was still home, with these two women there, the one who had conceived me and carried me inside her, and the one who had seen me come out. If I insist on these first facts so much, it's because I'm no longer living with Paul. Otherwise, I'd think it exaggerated.

Now that Paul is sleeping with somebody else, under another roof, the whole question of home has become important to me. So my mother's new flat in the glass city, which wasn't my home, became my home simply because it contained the two people in the world who were closest to me, not counting Pauline and Paul. I don't believe a home is a question of walls.

For the first seven mornings I found Mother there in the new flat waiting for me with her usual patience. On the eighth morning I arrived and she was no longer there. Aunt Tanya opened the door to me. The second door, the one into Mother's room was closed, presumably in order not to shock me. That's so like my Aunt: as if the few seconds of being protected from what I was about to discover could change something. During the night Mother had vomited bananas, cream cheese and then blood, a lot of blood. At dawn they had taken her off to hospital. In socialist countries emergencies are dealt with quickly. For me, in the space of those few seconds, which Aunt Tanya had wanted to give me by keeping the door shut, Mother died.

Zelenograd is all mirrors and open spaces. You cross it by bus. The streets, as in New York, have numbers instead of names. This makes a difference. No more addresses commemorating the Red Army, or the 25th of October, or Lenin. The numbers of the buildings, for no apparent reason, are astronomically high. A kind of architectural space-fiction, reminding me of some of the Saturday-afternoon-films on television which Pauline watches, lying on the floor, far away in France.

In a pine forest at the edge of the city, we come to a hospital which is as white as virgin snow. This is where I'm supposed to find what is left to me of Xenia who is vomiting blood. I leave my Aunt and my sister-in-law at the door. For someone so gravely ill, only one person has the right to visit; and today this person is Xenia's daughter, who has come thousands of miles from Paris to see her.

I take off my coat, my boots, my scarf. I slip on some white canvas boots over my tights. Clutching my handbag which is too big, and in which I carry all my treasures, I climb up to the fifth floor and enter room 569. There are four beds. And there is Mother, not far from the door, her two arms attached to drips for serum and blood. By her lips, I can see that she's speaking to me, but I can't hear her. I move my ear closer. 'My adorable little doll,' she manages to say. Straight away I start to cry, despite all the promises I have made to myself. For my weakness, I blame Paul or perhaps this snarling bitch of a life. That Mother, in the state she was, should say such sweet things was too much. 'Take care of Paul,' she adds softly, 'and do up that button.' I do up the shirt button which her eyes indicate.

About Paul, I keep quiet. I tell her nothing about Paul. Because he's Paul, he's always there, like Pauline. Paul—Pauline—Liola. Mother used to say that we three, the trio of us, were her greatest joy on earth. I wanted to keep this intact for her. Not a word, not even a whisper. I turn my eyes away and dab at my tears, tears which have been so rare the last three years. Crying was something I un-learned, thanks to Paul.

Clear-sighted now, I look only at the bloodstained dressing around her elbow and at her white face on the flat pillow. Her face is still alive, it moves, it lifts itself up and changes its angle on the flat pillow. Mother never liked flat pillows. In bed she usually had two, three, several pillows, and never flat ones, they were always puffed up. Four taps with the back of her hand and she had a pillow puffed up. And I learnt to do the same. Economic gestures are one of the things she has bequeathed to me. These gestures have become like prayers. I cut onions like her, roll out pastry like her, I get pleasure like her from watching people eat.

She wasn't really there that day, she was leaving, moving away towards death, very quickly and all-too-clearly. I was to stay behind, holding the life-line. I was strengthened a little by the fact that—in her eyes at least—I was strong enough to do this. To me, it was less clear. I felt myself slipping away, drop by drop, with the blood she was losing. I was dying too and the blood I was losing was Paul. Paul, who was still interminably leaving me. It's strange how long some people take to leave you.

In fact I'm not sure whether I was thinking of Paul as I watched Mother struggling to live. She was dying. Paul had nothing to do with it, nor did Pauline. On my return I would tell Pauline nothing about the agony Mother was suffering. Pauline with her freckles and turned-up nose was eleven years old, but she had lived through the last stage with Paul in utter panic. Why do I bring everything back to Paul? It's unnecessary. Sitting in the chair, looking at Mother and the snow and the pine trees through the large window with scarlet curtains, a tap dripping somewhere behind me, and the blood-stained rag around Mother's arm, I nonetheless return to Paul without really meaning to.

One day Pauline will be sitting here, Pauline married, already a mother. It will be my turn to leave. She will be looking at me as I am now looking at Mother. That idea has for me something wonderfully normal about it. It is astonishing how much I love the normal.

The spring comes after winter. Christmas comes regardless of what one does. It is a certainty. And this is what I love. I dampen a handkerchief and wet Mother's lips with it. She is not allowed to drink.

Mother isn't complaining, which is hardly surprising given all the drugs they have pumped into her. But her strength is so much on the wane that it must be painful. Not even to have the strength to suffer, to regret, to get into a rage—that is a sure sign of a life on the ebb. That much I know.

Paul had managed to make me understand that he lived only for one woman, and that woman wasn't me. He had succeeded in doing this by writing. When he puts his mind to it, Paul writes better than anyone else.

I see myself on the landing of the house at Gif. Pauline was at school. I was beginning to cut up a bedcover, a bedcover of white cotton circles crocheted together, which Mother had given me. It was a masterpiece. And I was cutting it up, destroying it, white circle by white circle, with the same intensity as

Mother had put into the making of it. I was mad with pain and I had almost nothing to hold on to. Here, face to face with Mother, I certainly have something to hold on to.

One year, just one short year after the day on the landing with the bedcover, I was walking with a man beside the railings of the Luxembourg Gardens. It was autumn and everywhere there were dead leaves. In my last novel there had been a similar scene: a man and a woman, Jeanne and Alexander, walking beside the railings of the Summer Gardens in Petersburg. I wanted to write more about how happy my Jeanne was to be doing just that, just walking and scuffling the dry leaves. But I told myself: Liola, forget it! The dead leaves, the park railings, it's a bit too much, isn't it?

Suddenly now those other kind of leaves, the leaves of typing paper which I had thrown into the wastepaper basket were blown back to me. At my feet were the dead leaves of the trees in the Luxembourg Gardens, and beside me there were a man's blue eyes under a cap.

Everything in me awoke. I was at home again in time; I could remember things.

On the day of the bedcover, time had ceased to exist for me, I felt it no more than I felt anything else. Kostia, the man with the cap, was carrying a case full of manuscripts which he hesitated to publish in Moscow. As for me, I was incapable of writing any more. Censorship, prohibitions, obstacles, they come in different guises.

I collect all these obstacles and look at them, and place them like pebbles by the side of the road, just like in the story of Tom Thumb. When I do not know how to go on, I can see all the pebbles along the way I've come. It's over Paul that I stumble most. Yet time and again the very act of stumbling brings me back to life, reminding me of the blood and the salt which flows through our veins and which will go on doing so for as long as we live. The salt which is free to choose, which flows or which hardens, and which holds us together.

The bottle of blood was emptying itself and

this was a proof that Mother was alive. Her face, anyway, was less pale than the night before. Even in her old age Mother had a smooth skin with freckles like Pauline. What wrinkles faces, I think, is spitefulness, intolerances, jealousy, the desire to possess, a lack of goodness. I'm not thinking of the ordinary wrinkles of the skin, but of ravaged faces, faces whose expression and spirit are like a ruin.

When I was little I was always losing my ribbons, they slipped out of my too fine, too straight hair. This complicated Mother's budget. She used to scold me too about my gloves, I was always losing one glove and then the other was useless. About my scarves too, which I left everywhere. Later she used to scold me about my trousers. Even when it was cold, I refused to wear them. The trousers had to be seen to be believed. They transformed you into a shapeless woollen doll, like the kind you put over a teapot to keep it warm.

Finally I had to put on the trousers since Mother couldn't be argued with on this point.

11

But no sooner out of the door, than I hid them under the cellar stairs. One day the cellar got flooded and the trousers disappeared, they were carried away by the current. That was a memorable day, not one of my happier ones. I can understand Mother now: it was no joke trying to find a warm garment in the shops during a socialist winter.

I can't bring myself to scold Pauline when she treats her clothes just as badly as I did. She loses and dirties her clothes as easily as she breathes. She comes in with a pair of jeans hopelessly torn and then it's I who have to console *her*. Her tears encourage mine and we both end up by crying.

But since Paul left the house in Gif, I never cry openly. Paul says that when he first knew me in Moscow, I used to cry in trams, in parks, in railway stations, in swimming pools, in telephone booths, museums, aeroplanes, corridors. He is exaggerating as usual—it's one of his charms.

Paul and I met in Moscow a long time ago. I was wearing a dress that Mother had made for me out of a remnant—it was blue with little white flowers—which had probably been intended for something like a pillow case. Not at all smart, yet I liked it very much. It was the month of July. At five o'clock every morning, I left home to travel sixty kilometres, first by train and then by bus. My brother, Genia, had found me a job and this earned me a few hundred roubles a month. The money was going to stop Mother worrying. She was worried because in the autumn I was going into my fourth year at the philosophy faculty and I had no shoes. There was also the problem of a winter coat. The winter before, she had managed to get the padding and the lining; now it was a question of buying the cloth itself.

That summer I used to carry a book by a Belgian philosopher in a string bag. I had to review it for *Problems of Philosophy*. In the train and in the bus, I slept sitting up. I was getting nowhere with the book. On the construction site, where my brother was manager, my job was to note down all the workers present and

13

absent. Then I slept standing up. Sometimes I used to go and sleep, stretched out in the Ostankino Park near the building site; it was a way of profitting from the weaknesses of the socialist economy. Then came the lunch break. Usually I went to have whatever was on the day's menu, and a glass of tea, in the Ostankino Restaurant. That's where I saw Paul for the first time, or, more accurately, where Paul saw me. From the day of my birth I've been as short-sighted as a mole, and up till then I refused to wear glasses, preferring to live in a haze.

I get up to adjust Mother's arm, it has fallen off the edge of the bed. By accident, my elbow rubs against her chest and it hurts her as much as if I had hit her. Even the thin blanket of this over-heated hospital is an intolerable weight for her. The drug is wearing off, the injection isn't working any more. I go into the hall to find a nurse. I empty the chamber pot which also has mucus and blood in it. We all contain litres of blood, normally we don't think about it, we are only aware of it when we're losing it, when we are losing blood or love.

Mother asks me to cover her. She has had another injection. I make the gesture of tucking her in, just as I do at Gif in the evenings for Pauline. Mother doesn't like it. In Russia you never tuck the sheet under the mattress. It's left loose and you roll yourself up in it. I was forgetting.

Seeing Mother refuse the tucked-in sheet, I remember how I instinctively rediscovered that way of rolling yourself in, of swaddling yourself in the bedclothes, as soon as Paul had gone for good from my bed. This made me think about Paul's warmth again. Even now, in the debris of the shipwreck which he so carefully organized, it's impossible for me to deny Paul's warmth; that warmth which was part of my very first impression of him.

I was finishing a cutlet in the Ostankino Restaurant. I could hazily make out some ten people sitting at a reserved table. Right in the middle of the table there was a red, white and blue flag on a miniature flagpole, planted in an iron stand. Frenchmen. All of them were intent on reading the menus from top to bottom, those menus which promise everything that the culinary art of communism might produce if imagination and science were combined. The choice ranged from octopus in sea-kale to partridge in bilberries, passing by the famous 'Kasha Gourieff'. So many extinct gastronomical species! I knew very well that those menus were a form of epitaph, a purely verbal homage to pre-1913 Russian cuisine. Yet peering at the poor famished Frenchmen, I told myself that perhaps, just for them, a miracle would be produced.

The waitress came to take their orders, and firmly announced that no attention whatsoever should be paid to what was printed—that was literature. The eatable food, the available food, was listed on a little piece of loose paper attached to the cover of the menu with a clip.

I had the impression that the Frenchmen had taken in the bad news, but that in order to amuse themselves a little, they were pretending not to understand so that the waitress would have to repeat her speech all over again. She was out of her depth. That's when I intervened. Perhaps I used a somewhat peculiar French, influenced by my Belgian philosopher's thinking about Hegel. Anyway, I provoked an outburst of laughter such as I had never heard or seen in sober adults. They were choking. Savages! Under Stalin we had lost the habit of such scenes of impropriety in public places!

I paid my bill and was drinking my last sip of tea, when suddenly the little circle of Frenchmen, calm now, approached my table. I particularly noticed a man with badly cut black hair, a blue mediterranean fisherman's sweater and crumpled trousers. He bowed, took my hand and kissed it, as if we were in Madame de Guermantes' velvet drawing room. Nonplussed, I just had time to notice a few white hairs at his temples and a network of fine wrinkles near his eyes. Nobody kisses your hand in the Soviet Union and I could easily have found his gesture vulgar. I let it pass, perhaps because of those little signs of a man

17

getting on in age. No, let me be frank—it had more to do with the fact that somehow this man intrigued me. I could feel in him something that was both highly-strung and calm, something unusual which wasn't simply to be explained by the fact that he was from a different country. From the start, I felt that there might be a kinship between this stranger and myself.

I got up in my pillow-case dress, walked away and no longer gave the matter much thought. But at home in Kuntsevo that evening, while I was reading a new chapter on Hegel with the help of a dictionary, this stranger came back to me in a flash. Quickly I shut both my eyes and the dictionary, and I asked a secret question—Russian schoolgirls often do this. My eyes still closed, I opened the dictionary at random and let a finger land on the page. I opened my eyes to read the answer. To the left of my fingernail was the word 'Marriage'.

It wasn't a good summer for me. I had wanted to go to the Black Sea, but the

18

problem of my coat and shoes kept me to my building site. It was a cushy job, thanks to my brother Genia, but due to a lack of sleep, I felt too tired even to go to the Film Festival in Moscow, although I was mad about the cinema. Mother even thought that my nose was growing pinched—and this wasn't a good sign. Mother always paid a great deal of attention to the nose. For her it was a gauge of whether or not I was wasting away.

Now I am looking at Mother's nose and her sleeping face on the flat pillow. For somebody who has so little time before them, perhaps it is sad to sleep. Paul left behind in the house—on purpose or did he forget it?—a book on cancer which describes various methods of euthanasia. The most advanced and progressive methods. When the suffering is too much and there is no hope left, they kill you very gently: they inject you with cocktails which send you to sleep deliciously and forever. Some people don't like to be put to sleep in this way, especially children. They are the ones who fight most fiercely against going. As if they

19

knew that sleep has certain advantages over being awake, but only on condition that waking is guaranteed.

When Mother wasn't sleeping, she called for sleep, and when she felt sleep coming, she protested. And she protested so faintly that it hurt me, because, until then, she had always made what she wanted very clear, she always knew how to give orders and take command.

When, during the war, we left Moscow to go as refugees to a small lost village at the foot of the Urals, she saw to it that we took warm things with us: felt boots, duvets, thick coats. Her friends who were officer's wives, her Moscovite friends, did not think of taking anything except their fox furs and their crêpe de Chine dresses. And this made life difficult for them in a village where every morning you had to break snow with a shovel just to get out the door. It was a village of women and children, like us the ones from Moscow, and the ones who had always lived there. The men from the Moscow families and the men from the village families were all at the war. My father was at the Volkhov front near Leningrad.

During the time we spent in this village I retained three images from the past: an image of an ordinary orange, an image of a kind of ice cream which you put into a mould and it comes out rectangular between two wafers, and the image of a little bar of chocolate wrapped in silver paper. Image is the right word. I had forgotten the tastes. The time passed slowly. I spent hours sitting on the stove next to a very old man. He was the only grown-up member of the family where we were billetted. The rest of the family were ten or twelve years old, the age of my two brothers. This family of temporary orphans shared their new frozen potatoes with us. These potatoes were slightly sweet, not very good. I used to eat them with my mind's eye fixed on my three images: the orange, the ice cream and the chocolate.

These imaginary meals would then lead to another vision: that of the war being over. Men were coming home, above all my father

21

was coming home. In his arms he was holding the doll of my dreams: a plastic baby that I could bath. In the Moscow streets there were ice cream kiosks, coloured balloons. This vision of mine was distinguished by the total absence of snow, as if victory on the battle fields would bring in its train a complete change of weather. Confidence in this final victory was shared by both the peasants and the townswomen who were continually coming to our house.

Mother knew how to read cards like no one else on that side of the Urals. She also knew, when necessary, exactly how to cover up her mistakes. She could cover up with anything. When her talents were rewarded, we had two or three eggs to go with our potatoes or sometimes even a tiny scrap of bacon. This happened above all when Mother predicted a leave and the man in question then came home. Came home not in a dream, but by road, having travelled a long way. Really came home. It didn't matter if he wasn't always a complete man—a limb or some other part might be missing—but it was still him. In the village all the women were waiting for their men, whole or not.

I was waiting for mine. I was already one of the women. I waited with such longing that he finally came, without his right arm but with my doll. Later Mother told me that I hid under the bed, Father couldn't get me out, I shouted that I didn't love him any more. And then—as was bound to happen—I left my place under the bed, left the warmth of the stove and spent days and nights on his knees. He had both knees. I don't want to draw any comparisons between childhood and maturity on the subject of how the man you love is absent and then returns. I'd rather believe that one can always keep a certain presence of mind.

At last the war ended and, as in my dreams, the snow did melt. Though it came back. We were in Moscow, Father was there. I remember the whole sky. It was as multi-coloured as a rainbow and even more beautiful. There were rockets of every kind, as if all the world's flowers had met in the sky. I was perched on Father's shoulders and I was licking a strawberry ice cream. I watched the German prisoners file by. I learnt later that this idea of having them file past us like trapped animals was Stalin's. They weren't at all as I had imagined. They were ashen and in rags. I felt a great shame; my father said nothing. The crowd stood there amazed and silent and you could hear the muffled plodding of thousands of bare or bandaged feet.

Mother bequeathed me her round nose. All the rest of me is Father's. The nose is frivolous, up in the air. Tonight as I watch her sleeping on the flat pillow, Mother's nose has effectively grown longer, as if pinched. Death is already doing his work, modelling her nose in his own image. She always had small hands, now they are even smaller, for she has grown so thin during the last year. One of her arms lies across her chest. The other arm would be there too if it weren't held to one side by the drip. When I go to sleep without Paul, I cross my arms over my chest as though I were embracing myself. What time can it be? In the ward only a night light is burning. I'm not sleepy.

Vladimir Petrovitch, the surgeon on duty, told me this morning that he would come and take me away for a moment, that we could have tea together. When? He didn't know. It depended upon the condition of a patient he was about to operate on. He told me that my idea of spending the night here with my mother was not very clever; and that, in any case, it was not allowed. "Just one night, Vladimir Petrovitch, one short night, the last one."

He listened without listening, as if he had foreseen what I was going to say. As he walked away, he said, "If I may, I'll come and find you tonight." My country is like that. People spend their lives getting round what is forbidden.

Mother used to make my dresses, as she did everything I wore. A little surprisingly, she always wanted my dresses to mould my hips. She saw no harm in that. At least that's the

25

way it was from the day I had any hips. The line of her life and my hips were somehow linked.

In the dim light of the single bulb, thoughts come and dance in my head. In my memory I watch one of my own private films of the sixties. Jean-Luc was a friend of Paul's in those days. In the house at Gif I have a photo of Jean-Luc, without his glasses. He is lying on some crumpled sheets, a little as if he were floating on white waves. I often look at this photo. With no glasses, his eyes are melancholy, bewildered. Nothing protects him. When he was struggling with his real films, he used to call me Apple. Then came the year of the Chinoiseries, and he no longer called me Apple because I wasn't Chinese. I think he even held it against me that I wasn't Chinese. One day he came to the house, as usual, without warning. That day Pauline had spilt a large pot of oil paint over her head. I have never quite understood how she did this, because she was scarcely bigger than the heavy paint pot. I spent all the afternoon

26

trying to clean her up with almond oil. There was still paint in her ears, her nose, the corners of her eyes. Not long before, Paul had hidden Pauline under his overcoat and taken her to see *Pierrot le Fou*. So I turned to Jean-Luc and said: 'It's all your fault!'

At that time the cinema was one of Paul's passions and I used to go to films with him. On the pavement, on the side of the Champs Elysées with odd numbers, we met Jean-Luc. His black overcoat made him look very thin, dark glasses protected his eyes, glasses which in the winter night gave him something of the air of a gangster. He scarcely ever unclenched his teeth or laughed, but when he did laugh, it was like a miracle. He liked pasta, cakes and fast silent cars. Once he lent me one of those cars. I shouldn't have taken it, for it exploded half-way up the Boulevard Raspail. Now I no longer know what Jean-Luc likes. He's not around any more. As for Paul's likes and dislikes, insofar as I know them, they leave me cold. I can do nothing about it.

At night faces you have forgotten during

the day come back. I'm no specialist in insomnia. I sleep, regardless, my arms crossed over my chest, still confident that I'm going to wake up. In the past I didn't think about any of this. Life went on of its own accord, quietly. Paul, the night-time, the daytime, Jean-Luc's films, potatoes baked in the oven, Mother and Father telephoning from Moscow asking me to come and see them, Pauline learning to talk, summertime in the little house lent to us by my friend Fenosa in San Vincent in Catalonia. I didn't look for any explanations. What went on inside me barely interested me, I only noticed the gestures and acts of others: Jean-Luc's rare smiles, Sonia's coughing fits which were beginning to get worse in the year of the Chinoiseries, Paul seeing less and less of Jean-Luc, Sonia and I trying to find out why she coughed with such terrible violence when in principle there was nothing the matter with her lungs. Yet life still went on. The tempo of my second book was inevitably that of a waltz. One, two, three! The feet of Jeanne, the heroine, come together in one

28

place on the floor of the dance hall, before being swept away to another.

Nothing comes effortlessly any more. That is finished. In the morning, I insist upon going through the list of my hopes, the full list. But during the course of the day, they get scattered. Day after day I change myself into a soldier who fights for a purpose, who has to invent a sense for things. Going on living is a series of battles, some of which I lose.

On a beach on the Costa Dorada, where I still go for the summers with Pauline, there are some flowers called sand lilies. Delicate and white, these flowers possess a rare insolence. They grow out of the rubbish daily left behind by campers and, on Sundays, by people from Barcelona: they grow through opened, jagged sardine tins, through beer bottles full of sand, through packets of Ducados cigarettes, rotten fruit, plastic bags. The sand lilies are stubborn, they flower, and each summer they are more numerous and more sweetly perfumed.

Fenosa, who was born in the nineteenth

century, had a grandfather on his father's side who was a lamplighter. He is a sculptor. His sculptures, called little Fenosas or big Fenosas, as if they were the children and grandchildren of a family, are mostly of women. Fire women, cloud women, sun women, storm women. He takes a little moist clay and makes women for himself. With the tips of his trembling fingers, he caresses the forming shape. Then he takes off the excess clay with a seashell. These figures, like flowers shipped over long distances, are put to sleep in flat boxes. Later they're changed into bronzes so that they will die less soon.

Sometimes it happened that I took hold of some sand lilies and squeezed them tightly, unable to let them go. I brought them back from the beach and placed them in a glass of water in front of Fenosa. They kept us company while we ate salted cod and tomatoes. Fenosa has no sense of thrift except where speech is concerned. I feel happy near him. His eyes are always saying something. So too are his hands, his hair, his soul, his clay women. But out loud, Fenosa says almost nothing. This time, the sand lilies did make him utter more than three words. 'Given the way they've begun, these flowers will go far,' he said. 'Men, trees, birds, will vanish. The world will no longer be habitable for them. Swallows are already disappearing. These days you see only martins flying at dusk and they are stronger, but they too will vanish. Only those flowers, those lilies, will stay. They'll people the planet. They'll build towns with many fountains!'

Fenosa is right. The sand lilies have courage and many talents. Yet near them, on the beach, I once saw a mother looking after her child in a deck chair. He had skeletal legs, the legs of Treblinka. The patience with which the mother constantly moved those legs so that they could benefit from the sun was beyond reason. She believed she could bring them back to life, that one day they would grow muscles and walk like other legs. To me her faith was even stronger than the capacity of the sand lilies to draw up water from the

31

depths of the sand. Her faith was much, much stronger.

I won't admit that Mother is no longer believing me when I tell her that she will see the Spring, and that Pauline will come and visit her. In a similar way, somewhere inside me, I won't admit that I've lost Paul.

It's when I'm ill in bed, when I have a high temperature, that I have the most common sense. I make myself consider the empty space beside me. I say to myself that the space wouldn't be less empty if I were a widow. Does this comfort me? No, it doesn't. And then I tell myself frankly: it is essential in life to learn to endure absences; to prepare oneself for the death of others, for one's own death. A little training so that the big moments of reckoning are not too shocking.

Meanwhile there is still the lilac, its flowers coming through the window, and there is Pauline who comes up the stairs each morning. How does she know that I am so fragile in the morning? She does nothing to upset me, she doesn't even say anything silly which might make me smile. From where did she get this gift?

When I was Pauline's age and had to be woken up to go to school, Mother did all she could to make the shift from night to day easy for me, especially in the winter. I was asleep when she pulled on my stockings. My eyes were still closed when she did my hair. As she put on my knickers, my shirt, my skirt, I gradually found myself in a standing position. And there was my tea waiting. I rubbed my eyes. Mother stirred the spoon in the cup to make the sugar dissolve. She kissed me rarely. Her acts took the place of kisses.

Did Mother believe in God? I asked her one day in Zelenograd. She made a gesture with her hand, a gesture which didn't mean anything at all, and then she looked at the wall. How well I remember one morning, just after the first night when Mother, Paul and I slept in the same room, Mother on her bed, and I with him on the sofa. Paul left for work very early and I began to cry. Mother came and sat next to me, took me in her arms and said, 'It's beautiful when you love one another. The most beautiful thing that can happen to anyone when you love one another.'

Mother had a weakness for Paul. I saw this. The pancakes she made him eat in the morning were particularly inspired. I was well placed to judge. Paul wore neither tie nor suit, not even his overcoat accorded with her ideas. At first she despaired of the fact that he looked like a tramp. Then she accepted it.

When I am writing, it almost seems as if I'm not. I write slowly, just putting one foot in front of the other. I take my time in order to find out. Find out what? I'm somebody who can't be rushed. Pauline knows that. Mother and Father knew it. Yet suddenly on the stairs, Paul turned round and said point blank, 'I'm haunted by the image of a woman I've met. I can't get her out of my mind.'

Somewhere between the age of twelve and sixteen, we go through a woolly period. The wool muffles the world, as if to make the changes taking place in us less painful. The capacity to forget is wonderful then. Pauline, still little, hasn't reached this period yet. But I went through it again, a kind of delayed reaction. If I hadn't, I couldn't have gone on.

Paul took trains, went, came back. He and the woman who haunted him were waiting to love one another openly. I behaved as if all this were the most natural thing in the world. In newspapers, in books, everywhere, there was only the supreme power of Sexual Desire, as celebrated by the analysts. In Paris people were freeing themselves, just as they were in other capitals. And I, a Russian, a provincial in these matters, I tried to escape to somewhere within myself. There I wasn't altogether alone. I made myself work. Jeanne, the young woman in my novel, helped me. She proved her worth. I piled sorrow after sorrow upon her, abandonment after abandonment, to see how she would face up to it all.

I remember I was typing the last pages of a chapter: it was about Russia during the civil war. Jeanne was searching everywhere for Alexander, her man, her lover. A ray of sunshine fell on my back, warming it, and for the first time since Paul had been 'haunted', I had a sense of well-being. It was only a ray of sunshine, nothing to dance about.

I never again want to see Paul dancing in the sunshine at Barcelona airport by the fountain and the giant clock. Sonia was going back to Paris, Paul was arriving the same day at almost the same time. Pauline was there, looking like a peach with her red hair and golden cheeks. Pauline was still young enough to be happy wearing dresses. I was talking with Sonia. She made a sign with her eyes and I turned round to see Paul dancing by the fountain with Pauline in his arms. The sunlight, coming through the airport windows, was streaming down on them.

Yet I was still good for something. I could still go on writing about Jeanne's life, because my other memories vanished before this one of Paul waltzing with Pauline. And another one too: the image of Pauline's face when I saw her for the first time. I had been put to sleep for the caesarean. When I woke up, Pauline was there, wrapped in white, her face framed by a bonnet. She was fresh and rested: caesareans have at least that advantage. For me there can be no face more beautiful than that of Pauline's on her first day of life. Yes, all mothers say this. But I stress it, I think, to reaffirm what belongs to us for ever, our only happiness on this earth, a handful of moments, the waltz by the fountain for example, and Pauline's face on her first day.

For a long time Pauline refused to speak. She was neither deaf nor blind, she had everything she needed and in the right place. I didn't worry. After all, she heard her mother speaking Russian to her friends and Sonia speaking Armenian on the telephone, she heard Spanish and Portuguese being spoken by the young women minding the children in the park, and everything else was said in French. She was a little lost in the midst of all this. At last, one winter night around three or four in the morning, she deigned to speak. She wasn't sleeping and Sonia, who only slept in the daytime for a few hours, was holding Pauline in her arms by the window. Pauline pointed a finger toward the trees and said: 'Someone black.' She said it calmly, intelligibly, thoughtfully, without a trace of a Russian or any other accent, and with nothing childish in her tone.

After this forbidding beginning, her mind focused on prehistoric monsters. Paul brought her picture books full of saurians. Models of dinosaurs, ichthyosaurs and other prehistoric lizard-like animals were her only toys. She spent hours gazing at highly coloured, very lifelike pictures of these creatures: their long slack bodies rising from the mud in the midst of giant flowers, their tiny heads lost in the sky amidst flying reptiles. Once more I am looking over Pauline's shoulder at these creatures and once more I am struck by their gaze. In man and animal everything depends upon the look in the eyes, and in their reconstructions from fossil evidence, the painters of these pictures were able to recreate all the secondary components of these animals, but not the look in their eyes, and so their eyes didn't exist. They were absent eyes. Like the absent look in the eyes of the polio-ridden child on the Catalonian beach; like Mother's eyes when she blankly noticed the bouquet of snowdrops I'd placed on her bedside table; or that look I sometimes catch in Fenosa's eyes when his vocal cords betray him and he can't quite put into words one of his thoughts about the stars.

Leaping in one bound over the entire history of the earth, Pauline passed without any transition from the gaze of the ichthyosaurus to science fiction. Films like *Close Encounters of the Third Kind* she saw at least ten times. I went with her once. She wanted me to. Clinging grimly to the armrests, she no longer moved or breathed. In the dark, her eyes shone brighter than the stars on the screen. At the climax, when the saucer arrived, they were full of tears. Though I found the giant saucer and its music very beautiful, I did not understand why so many people should suddenly find themselves so involved in the image of a sacred, truncated mountain they had never seen. I told Pauline so. She looked at me indulgently for a long while, then took my hand, made me sit down and talked to me about dreams, intuition, mediums—a whole little course in parapsychology. Sometimes she stopped to ask me whether I understood. Her knowledge impressed me less than the naturalness, without disappointment or contempt, with which she wanted to make good my ignorance.

Doctor Jung says somewhere that the most deeply buried fibres of our psychic life may be vestiges of ancient nervous systems—like those of the lobsters—or of spinal marrow originating millenia ago in the dinosaurs. I think sometimes that this must be what Paul touched in me—these fibres of a primordial past. That might explain why I am unable to forget him or the one who haunts him.

I suddenly woke in the dark and could just make out Paul sitting by the bed doubled up. I thought it must be a toothache, a liver attack. But no. He was being haunted. He admitted it, and then added, 'It's nothing.' For a long time I thought I had a special task. I had to help Paul, I had to try to understand him. Yet in return, he made me feel that Pauline and I were simply obstacles in his way. And so I changed tack. I bought the most beautiful flowers in the market at Gif. I was such a good customer that they used to give me flowers on top of what I'd bought. I wore pretty white dresses which I starched carefully. I made my hair soft and fluffy. I washed Pauline non-stop, which wasn't always easy. I did everything so that the two obstacles should at least be fresh, bright, perfumed and blossoming. In Paul's eyes I was doing this just in order to make the obstacles greater, to complicate his life yet further.

The period of being obstacles lasted about a year. Every day was very long. Time was suspended. The curtain on the next act went up early one morning. Paul came home having spent the night in the company of the one who haunts him. He was out of his mind, delirious. He spoke to me as if I were not

41

myself but someone else. I felt guilty for not being this other person. The next day he regained his equilibrium and I packed his bag. Pauline and I ceased to exist as obstacles, and straightaway we had more air to breathe, more space in the house. I thought it would be easier to live with someone who was truly absent.

But no, the one who was absent didn't absent himself. Paul no longer spent the nights at Gif, but he came back every day, like a sleepwalker. He would sit down on the kitchen floor and mend Pauline's old toys. He would bring a whole collection of new light bulbs to replace just one that he had noticed was burnt out. Soon after he came with some very beautiful candelabra and yards of electric wires. It's hard to say which I felt more strongly—exasperation at seeing him drifting about in this way, or pity, an affectionate pity, because he was behaving as though, as a result of his departure, Pauline and I were bound to be plunged into darkness.

His attentions upset me. I decided that I

had to be finished with him. For the first time in my life, my health preoccupied me. I had to go on living at whatever cost, for Pauline's sake. I needed a certain freedom to recover my balance, to make a clean sweep. I wanted to banish words like Feeling, Passion, and the like, from my vocabulary. Paul was stopping me from doing so. He found a kind of solace in feeling guilty. He was bent on proving to me that the years we had spent together had created bonds which survived catastrophes. On each of his visits, he referred to these bonds. There is no one who drives in nails more persistently than Paul when he puts his mind to it. In the middle of January he started to embellish his 'bonds' with roses and white lilac. His bonds were becoming too much for me. The motto of Paul Morand's character, the man-who-was-always-in-a-hurry, came to my mind: his motto was 'Quickly and Badly'. Did Paul want to live out all his tragedies that quickly during one lifetime?

'It doesn't seem to be going well for you Paul,' I ventured to say while arranging some

43

flowers in a vase. 'Why should things go well?'
he replied in a simple voice as if the search for
happiness was a fool's game. Yet fool's game
or not, I could read Paul almost like a book.
He was in a mess, that is all there was to it. He
got up to straighten an icon that was hanging
a little crookedly on the wall, and then went
and stared through the window at the walnut
tree in the neighbour's garden: a tree that he
had always liked. Without turning towards
me and in the same simple voice, he said: 'To
come and live with me, you didn't have to
leave anyone.'

That was true. There I had been lucky. My
only worry then was about earning enough
roubles to buy the winter coat and shoes, so
that I could go to the university in a
temperature of twenty degrees below zero. I
used to call those pennies I earned on the
building site my penance. I would say to Paul:
'I earned extra penance today' or: 'No work, no
penance.' It was a slip, pure and simple. I had
the two words confused. Before learning the
word pennies, I knew the word penance,

having read it several times in texts on moral philosophy.

Monad—another philosophical term—was more familiar to me than 'promenade' and I would say, 'Let's take a little monad.' I'm sure a lot of people who learn a foreign language make mistakes like this at the beginning. Paul used to make fun of these slips of mine. On the first of January he wrote to me from Paris: 'For others the year is beginning now. For me it began in the summer, during the days of penance.' Paul can give anything a halo of spirituality. Since he stopped living at Gif, he never fails when he comes into the house to take off his shoes, as if he were crossing the threshold of a mosque.

I turn the shoes over. The soles have holes. He has a special way of walking, a little like Chaplin in *City Lights*. Fashionable shoes aren't meant for that. He has holes in his shoes barely a few hours after buying them, and always in exactly the same place. And then he goes on wearing them even in rain or snow. Those holes used to hurt me. As soon as I had

earned some royalties, I bought Paul two
spare pairs of shoes. That way he would have
dry feet for at least a few hours. Now there are
other holes which have hurt me. When Paul
leaves the house, that makes a hole.

No sooner does he arrive than he has to
leave. It's invariable. His arrival signals his
departure. I've worked out a whole system of
warnings and counter-warnings for myself.
But it does no good: the imminence of each of
his departures pushes me to a cliff edge. I look
down into space and I suffer a kind of vertigo.
It soon passes with a hot water bottle or a
vinegar compress on the heart, but I am
always obliged to lie down. When the moment
for departure arrives—and it may be at any
time—it is like an event ordained by fate:
obediently he puts on his shoes and does his
best to leave the house without being noticed.
Sometimes I only know he is leaving because I
hear Pauline, from downstairs where she is
watching the television, shout out: 'See you
later, Dad!'

My friend Nastia, who works on hormone

research, tends toward a hormonal explanation of Paul's behaviour. When it was a question of saying, 'I have to leave you and I will,' Paul found a far less direct, a more subtle way of saying it. Indeed it was only his slightly hoarse voice which lent any drama to his words at all. Yet, in reality, Pauline and I could never have been more dramatically left, more thoroughly abandoned, than we were in our state of polite doubt. The politeness meant that Paul had no bad conscience about not being there; his absences did not trouble him. It also meant that Pauline and I were placed in a state of constant confusion concerning his presence and absence. For him to feel good, we had to go out of our minds. Was he perhaps asking too much of us? One evening, while he was taking the air by the open window, I picked up a large vase of flowers and threw it at his head. Undoubtedly my strain of gypsy blood was in revolt and had sought some aid from the dinosaurs and lobsters.

Violence distresses Paul. He can't stand it. 'Now you are going too far.' He admonished me in a courteous but strained voice, while wiping his face and looking out of the corner of his eye to check whether the vase I had broken was his favourite, the white porcelain one with tiny blue flowers. I've rarely known anyone so unpossessive about property as Paul, but when he's thinking, he likes to let his eyes fall on a small number of familiar and simple objects. The white porcelain vase with blue flowers, if not Pauline and I, figured among these objects.

So as not to be throwing vases at him every day, I called on the fundamental patience of the Russian people as embodied in their popular proverbs. That time a more violent proverb came into my mind. 'When the head of somebody is cut off, you no longer mourn his hair.' I could fling all the vases in the world at Paul, I could apply every Russian proverb to his behaviour, he would still continue as before, along the path he had chosen. This inexorability was something I was going to have to admit.

I don't know why I was always washing

myself, I bathed, I showered, I sprinkled. Was I trying to lather myself away? A kind of dissolution? Despite her protests, I washed Pauline too.

I drank water. I ate nothing. 'You've fallen in love,' Nastia said when she saw my jeans flapping around me like a cobbler's apron. 'I'm going to give you some antasthene shots.' Pharmaceutics to redeem ashes! No, it was better to laugh. For a moment, while cleaning the ears of Nastia's baby son with cotton wool on a match stick, I toyed with this unknown colourless word, 'antasthene'.

Nastia's son was called Vassia, after my father who had died that year. It had been a good idea of hers to have a baby somewhat late in life. A new face, new hair, a new voice, mischief, there's nothing like these for giving you a new sense of life. Now Vassia can walk, and tells me his own news over the telephone.

Nastia and Vassia slept at Gif on New Year's Eve. Paul was absent, holding the hand of the one who haunted him. Pauline was away in the mountains. Nastia was happy as a

49

lark. On New Year's morning, it was sunny. The house at Gif has a talent for catching the light. The sun was playing on the walls, the ceilings, the floor. We drank our coffee sitting on the carpet and listening to a Brazilian record which Pauline likes. Vassia asked for some hot chocolate. He drank a drop and spilled the rest on the carpet. Nastia's eyes darkened. I didn't move, I just looked at the chocolate sea and thought: it is happiness for me to have Nastia and Vassia here on New Year's Day.

Loss teaches us the order of things, I think. Once I wept just because Pauline broke the window of the front door. Paul's heart must have already been elsewhere, but I didn't know it. Any more than I knew what he meant when, one evening with friends at dinner, he suddenly said: 'Provided they don't take Liola away from us.' I blushed. I could not see what could possibly take me away from Paul, or Paul from me. Even later, when Paul spelt it out, I didn't at first believe what he said. Only my dreams knew better.

I think people separate long before they realize it. You still walk holding hands, but the path isn't the same one. At times Paul used to lose faith in himself and flounder. He didn't talk about it, but I could feel it happening. With my confidence which was enough for two, I tried to restore his confidence. Indirectly. I began to write books for him, as I would have made children for him. Yet in these books I lived in other places, brought to life other people. It seemed to Paul that I was escaping and he smelt betrayal.

In fact in writing a novel there is something of this: you leave, you take something away from somebody. You also kill a part of yourself even if at the same time you bring another part to life. Perhaps I did go a little fast. I felt loss stalking me and by writing I was trying to lure loss away, or at least make a place for it. There had been too many deaths in one fell swoop: Sonia's, Ludmilla's at Nice, my own father's. I felt a casting adrift, a fear. By telling stories, I tried to exorcize it.

At this time one of Pauline's phrases used to

come back to me again and again: 'It's not serious,' she would say. This was perhaps the second thing she ever said after 'Someone black'. Pauline broke clocks, telephones, loudspeakers, everything, and then she announced: 'It's not serious.' She knew how to give herself confidence. 'See you later,' she said when I left for Moscow. And now that her father no longer lives here, she says the same thing each time he goes through the door: 'See you later.' Pauline asks for no explanation and looks for no revenge. Her father loves another woman—it happens so often. She herself goes on loving him as before, without exuberance and apparently without any surprise at whether she sees him or not.

The religion of sexual desire, of 'sexual satisfaction'—a catch phrase of the time—makes me ponder. What is more ephemeral and capricious than Desire? It disturbed me to see Paul—when everything was still normal—fall for the magnetism of this new-found God, this God who prevented him from examining the stream of images filling his own mind.

At that moment Desire brought no images to my mind. But I saw it do so in others. Never before had I noticed men desiring me so insolently in the street. I realized that I could recognize their look, despite my short-sightedness, without even putting on my glasses. I also recognized the meaning of the smile on the lips of unaccompanied women, and the expression of the couples with their arms around one another in the park. For the first time in my life the spectacle of the world was clear to me, eloquent. It was as though a lucidity had replaced my short-sightedness. And this change worried me. I had often told myself that madness was nothing but an extreme lucidity, a lucidity without protection. Soon, thank God, my short-sightedness, both external and internal, returned.

If I look at the polaroid photos which Pauline took of me in those days, I find myself—why not use the word—radiant. Yet how furious I was when Paul, on one of his visits to the house, said to Pauline, who was proudly showing him these photos:

'But of course. Your mother is marvellous.'

It was then that I understood how women waste their time, at such critical moments, examining themselves in the mirror or asking whether it has happened because of their wrinkles, or their grey hair, or because their noses or breasts aren't perfectly shaped. Yet how to stop? You look for causes, for mistakes, for a way to do better. What else can you invent at such moments?

I keep mixing up periods in a happy-go-lucky way. Though that's hardly the phrase. The reader must have guessed that I'm not writing these pages for the beauty of the thing, but for other reasons. Or unreasons. Which?

Let's go on. I was trying to discover how to live with absence. With the presence of an absence, with the constant reminder in flesh and blood of an absence. Paul's constant comings and goings were creating havoc. Each time, I had to go round the whole circle again. He, in his triumphant innocence, could never have understood this. It would have been so much easier for me if I could have known that he was far away, on the other side of the ocean, or, if such a luxury was possible, at least in another city. I didn't dare go away myself because of Pauline. She liked the house, her school, her friends, our special neighbours, the garden.

There are people adept at forgetting. And Paul is one of them I think. An instinctive amnesia. Sometimes his lack of memory gets him into trouble. So one can hardly blame him if, at other times, he uses it to protect himself. Without the aid of this amnesia, how would he have been able to come and go, so easily, between his two homes? He did not want to hurt anyone. He thinks everyone is as forgetful as himself.

When I say 'he thinks', it's not quite right. Paul doesn't think. He acts. He moves. He circles in orbit around whatever attracts him, and the attraction illuminates him. The orbits may change but the illumination doesn't. He does everything passionately. At one moment he is attracted to Childhood, at another to the Immediate. At one moment he relearnt Latin

55

to decipher the text of Joan of Arc's two trials; at another he disappeared under photocopies of Blaise Pascal's manuscripts, cut into strips. These strips covered the floors in the house because Paul was looking for an order to them and he needed a panoramic perspective.

After Joan of Arc, I was winded; in face of Pascal, something in me snapped. I went to Madrid with Fenosa. He was having an exhibition there. Among other sculptures there was one of a man carrying a horse on his back. I came back sooner than expected. The telephone rang. It was the first time I heard the voice of the one Paul dreamt about: 'Is Paul there?' I answered that he wasn't. I wasn't lying. Paul was no longer in the house, even if he was. There was a ghost who was called Paul by habit and there were two obstacles, Pauline and Liola. All these characters were approaching the day of judgement. The voice of the one he dreamt about testified to this.

I watch Mother sleeping. Of all this story, she is ignorant. That at least is a

56

comforting thought. I smile. I surprise myself by smiling. I feel a tenderness take over and I am peaceful. It happens that these inexplicable states of peace come upon me. Unexpectedly. Sometimes they last quite a long while. Then I thank the unknown for the unknown, as if the sun's rays or the freshly-opened leaves were personally addressed to me. I shouldn't allow Paul so much importance, so that he even invades this hospital room where Mother is asleep. My forces are gathering strength and closing their ranks. Forward without Paul! When all is said and done, we loved each other so much, he and I, that I have something left to survive on. And now it is Mother, who has no strength left for anything, who is helping me.

She was already unwell last Christmas. She complained of her heart. The Russians wear this organ out. I didn't like the haste with which she wanted to hand over to me all the family photos and the bundle of letters from Paul. I wanted the home, where Mother and Father were living when I first left for France,

57

to last a long time yet. I wanted to bring Pauline there again. And it lasted, this home, for only a few months more.

Amongst the family photos there's one of Mother at my age. Her face is smooth, her hair neatly tied back by a scarf. She's wearing a pre-war dress, Deanna Durbin style—an actress who was popular in Russia then and now forgotten. Her Vassia was to come back from the front with one arm missing, with his back reduced to a pulp by shrapnel, and with head wounds. Sitting on his lap, I came to know his smell. It was mixture of cognac and *eau de cologne* from a bottle with a label on which there was the name of a Greek island which I can't remember. Before the war Father only drank on holidays. This was exceptional among a people who were already living under 'The Chief of Chiefs'. In another photo Father looks very smart in his new lieutenant-colonel's uniform. Stalin changed the cut of all military clothes, so that they looked again like Tsarist uniforms. In place of his arm, amputated at the shoulder, there is an artificial one. The very latest: perfect articulation, pure pigskin, creaking a bit. Father didn't usually wear it. When Pauline and I brought him a beautiful London-made three piece suit from Paris, he put on his artificial arm so that the sleeve would fall better. He forgot his arm one morning and Pauline, nodding towards a glass with Mother's denture in it, whispered, 'Grandma's teeth are there, but where has Grandpa's arm gone?'

Father's hair was white now. Despite his stroke, he still drank. As soon as he knew Pauline and I were coming, he went out with a string bag to buy things. For Pauline, a bear beating a drum and a frog that jumped. For me, caviar and Georgian white wine. For him, I had a bottle of whiskey and a pair of furry doe-skin boots. These boots he immediately christened, 'Bye Bye Youth'.

Tentatively I suggested that he should drink the whisky slowly. A wasted effort. I didn't want to annoy him too much. He never annoyed me. He got drunk mellowly. He talked about the war, about me as a little girl. Much to Pauline's surprise, he sang a duet with Mother. Pauline had never heard or seen a duet. In the song they sang, there was a couplet about the 'blue scarf that you wore on your darling shoulders' and another about a soldier at the front staring at the fire in the stove and thinking: 'It's not easy to reach you, and Death is a few steps away.'

Father always said he was incredibly lucky to be wounded. It was on the day of his thirty-third birthday. His friends had arranged a party for him in a dug-out. The alcohol was 90% proof. This was all there was to drink on the Leningrad front and the only way of keeping warm. Before the party began, Father was rehearsing the plans for a 'defensive attack' in the General Staff dug-out a few yards away. He and his fellow officers received the signal that everything was ready for the party. They ran across the few yards which were exposed to enemy fire. A bomb exploded. All of them were killed except Father.

'We both escaped,' Father once told me

when he had drunk some vodka. 'Death passed under our very noses and we are both alive!' He was referring to an illness I suffered a few months after the war started. About this illness I remember only what Father and Mother told me later. Icicles, it appears, were its cause. I would not stop eating icicles during the March of '41. They were everywhere, on the shutters of the house, along the pavillion in the square where Mother took me for walks. As soon as her back was turned, I started crunching them. One night I collapsed with a very high temperature and a throat so swollen I could scarcely breathe. Father was completing his studies in military strategy at the Lenin Academy in Moscow and we were living in the suburbs. My symptoms started to be alarming: blue spots appeared all over my body. There weren't many trains at night, so Father wrapped me in an eiderdown, picked me up in his arms and started running along the road with the idea of stopping the first car that came by. There weren't many cars either, and of the few that passed, none stopped. We were not in luck. The drivers who weren't stopping, had survived the purges, had the means to run a car, and they were driving at night towards Moscow from a suburb famous for its wealthy dashas—such people were bound to be shits. The minutes passed. I was turning bluer and bluer and breathing less and less. What could he do? Father had the right to be armed on account of his military studies, and so, clasping me in the eiderdown under one arm, he pulled out his revolver with the other and fired into the air. A car stopped. A few minutes later I was in the Botkin Hospital with a probe down my throat.

Any night without sleep is long. The new blood bottle is already half empty. Mother is very still, too still. Too much of her strength has left her. Too much? What am I trying to measure? Is 'too much' a reasonable quantity? Can one be abandoned 'too much'? Don't such things imply that the limit has already been reached?

One night last summer in Patmos there was a strong wind blowing. There were five of us, two men and three women waiting for a car. The two men, with their backs to the wind, put their arms around their women to protect them. I wasn't protected, but it was not important for I had a shawl which Paul had given me when I was expecting Pauline, a blue traditional Orenburg shawl. These shawls are still made in Russia despite state planning. We were happy, Pauline and I, on that island. I spent my mornings with Jeanne, typing in front of a window which looked out onto a pile of gravel where a terrace was being rebuilt. Pauline and my friend, Franca, went off to do sea-diving and to fish for sea urchins. I stayed alone, happy to be able to get on with my book and watch a family of cats. The mother cat had chosen the pile of gravel as a shelter for her young. One day she disappeared, taking her family with her. But she forgot one kitten. He was completely wild. I've never seen his like. Nevertheless, he had to eat. On a stone near his hole, I put a saucer of milk. In my absence he drank it. Each new saucer I then left made him braver. Eventually he became so bold that he came up to my window and stared in at me, but only when it was shut, never when it was open. He devoured the remains of his first New Zealand chicken—which I gave him—like a tiger.

Why were all provisions on Patmos imported from New Zealand? 'Strange correspondences exist,' said Pauline gravely, with a look of the Close Encounter kind, 'between islands.' Pauline adores both celestial and earthly maps. She can't be without an atlas any more than Paul can be without newspapers. Paul gets up like a shot in the morning, drinks his coffee and reads the morning papers in a café. This is why he can't take holidays. There was no question of his coming to the island. I took a firm grip of myself and started to breathe the Grecian air with which so much began; for instance, I never tired of hearing the word *apocalipsis*. We heard it constantly as we approached the sea in our bus full of women dressed in black, who crossed themselves at ever corner. At first I thought they were afraid of being flung into the ditch, but they were simply crossing themselves each time we passed a chapel.

It was on the isle of Patmos that Saint John received his revelations, in a cave not far from where we were staying.

'How did this man,' Pauline asked me, 'who you said was Jesus' favourite disciple, land up here? Patmos is a long way from Israel.'

I answered vaguely: 'Yes, a long way. It suited the Romans, who were lousy colonialists, to send him to Patmos, as far away as possible, to get rid of him.'

'Oh, I see,' said Pauline. 'Patmos is like Magadan.'

It did something to me to hear Pauline use that word. 'Yes Pauline, if you like it's a little like Magadan, but Magadan is even further away from Moscow than Patmos is from the Promised Land. The sky there isn't so blue or so clear. The earth stays frozen, even in summer. Frozen earth, frozen fog, glacial winds, grey sea, terrifying rocks. Everything has been arranged so that a man there feels he is at the end of the world, surrounded by enemies, forgotten by God. And he is both hungry and thirsty. A man? Countless men, as numerous as ants in an anthill. Saint John, you know, was lucky to be alone, surrounded by vineyards and fig trees. He could sit in his cool cave with his secretary and dictate his visions. He was free to eat or to fast. He could walk in the valley where the sheep graze. He was free to contemplate the sky or talk to his God. He was free.'

'Free—what does that mean, Liola?'

Pauline uses my first name whenever she wants to show that she feels independent. I stopped talking. A long silence. Pauline waited, meditated on my lack of an answer, came up close to me, kissed me and went away.

I look at the gravel. There is no kitten. The typewriter is silent. There it is. I'm at Magadan. I have lived within my imagination so many long hours at Magadan, spent so much time with the prisoners, they have so filled my heart and mind, that now I can see

66

with my own eyes how dawn breaks at Magadan: the black file of prisoners winding through the snow, the guards armed with rifles, the dogs. They come to Magadan from every corner of my country. The first circles are already behind them. Once arrived there, they have lost everything: everything, that is, that normally sustains you: family, children, loved ones. All that they have are their bodies—more or less alive—and their minds. The more one loses, the less one has to lose. And so, perhaps, the less one is afraid. The more one may be free. Prisons exist not only where there is the maximum of barbed wire and the most dogs. That madness which makes people imprison *themselves* may be cured by the Magadan snow. This is the terrifying paradox that Kostia expounded to me one afternoon in his little hotel bedroom facing Montparnasse cemetery.

Kostia met his mother at Magadan after fifteen years of separation. She had been freed, but she did not have the right to leave. She was in Magadan in forced residence. 'In

Moscow,' Kostia said, 'they were dying of fear. I had just come from there and I'd seen it. But here in Magadan, they talked calmly of everything, just as you and I might talk in Paris.'

Kostia described Magadan to me in geographical detail. I could feel that his words were now ready to go to the printers. But they were so compelling, so alive, that they made me think of Fenosa under his palm tree in the morning, modelling clay as naturally as he breathed.

At the time of the 'Moscow Spring' during a few months at the end of the fifties and the beginning of the sixties, Kostia was spoken of as 'the Russian Hemingway'. When I first met him, he was already beginning to change. A story of his, which I had just read, was nothing like Hemingway. It was a very short story which told of a chess game between chance partners on a train, but already Magadan was in it. I could feel it. They were pages written with the sensibility of a Proust by a man who had faced the Stalinist terror. For me when I first met him, Kostia was the author of those pages. He was sitting on the floor in a Moscow flat. On the table stood a bottle of English gin, a slab of black bread, and a tall tin in which dried fish were standing upright. These tins of fish are especially designed for eating in submarines. To find them in Moscow is as strange as it would be to find Volga caviar in Patmos. The flat belonged to Andrei and we were sitting in the kitchen. Andrei's wife was away on holiday and there wasn't much food. How distant that evening now seems, especially so because two of my friends who were there are no longer alive. Ludmila and Sonia are dead. Kostia sat on the floor and drank gin and said little. Mother and Father were looking after Pauline in the Kuntsevo flat. I, too, was drinking gin. Sonia wasn't coughing yet. Kostia was making her laugh. Nothing much happened, nothing much was said. It is like a landscape in a mist. Yet it was only seven years ago.

The man talking to me about Magadan in the hotel bedroom with the empty Schweppes bottles, overlooking the cemetery of Montaparnasse is the same Kostia. He is sitting on his bed. I'm sitting next to him in an armchair. The day before yesterday I packed Paul's bag. Yesterday I told Pauline that Paul was no longer going to sleep in the house. Today I have come back to life. It is many years since I've looked at a man, except Paul, as I look at Kostia now. Of the Kostia I knew in Moscow, I recognize only the eyes, their blue, their smile and their sadness. It's as if he has grown smaller, both his face and body. Yet he has a new moustache and a new haircut. His hair is longer and slightly wavy. The room seems very hot to me. We laugh, though there isn't so much to laugh about. To hell with time and difference! My Magadan brother and I have well and truly met again and we are drinking Schweppes in front of the Montparnasse cemetery.

It's not a cemetery I like, but then I don't like the cemeteries here. In Russia the earth rests lightly on the bodies of the dead, or so one imagines. Here all these vast blocks of stone are too heavy. They are monuments to a civilized, cultured death, to investment death. Nevertheless, the cemetery of Montparnasse isn't just a collection of stones for me. One day, as we walked along the path which leads to the windmill, Paul told me that his first child, a boy, was buried there. And Renée is there. Renée, to whom I owe a great deal, Renée, who in the early days guided me through the labyrinth of French conjugations, agreements and articles. Unfortunately neither my clowning throughout our Russian translation sessions, nor my vegetable soups, were able to help her in return. Renée had the temerity to stake everything on one man and she fell from a height of six storeys.

For Kostia Montparnasse is a virgin cemetery. Yet Magadan speaks to us both far more loudly than our different pasts. We have our losses in common, as well as our achievements. We Russians have all come out of Magadan. We sit there quietly sipping a non-alcoholic drink, sharing an agreement we could never define. Some time after that evening in

Andrei's flat Kostia gave up drinking. From that evening, he tells me, he remembers only one thing: the image of a young woman with chestnut eyes, wearing a simple well-cut dress, who laughed and kept her distance. I listen to him talking about this woman with interest, for a few months ago I left her skin. She was another Liola whom one day I will perhaps have to find again. As he goes on talking, I discover that Kostia lost himself too; before I did, at about the time of the dried fish for submarines, when he gave up drinking. When a Russian stops drinking, it's like becoming an outlaw. First he goes into hiding, then into exile. Kostia and I compare our exiles.

Sometimes this famous war which men and women wage against one another, makes me smile. The differences are so small compared to what we have in common. And from just a few differences, a kind of racism develops; everything then becomes the fault of the other race.

When I first met Paul, he had already lived, while I wasn't much, I was more like a project.

I felt very strongly what life might be like and I was an ideal spectator. Paul appeared to me to be not only a man, but a world. He belonged to the category of miracles. You aren't surprised by a miracle. You feel possessed and calmed by it. So this can happen! So it's normal. Paul was my marvellously normal man. Marvellous like his letters. These may have complicated the life of the KGB censors working in the Moscow Post Office, but to me they were a world, a whole new perspective, a spectacle I couldn't grow tired of. Yet, to a certain point I was to remain a spectator, as if things weren't really happening to me.

My short-sightedness may have something to do with it. People who see well don't think about seeing. So they can see less. For the short-sighted, for the really myopic, seeing itself is an act. And so they see more. The world is perhaps further away in terms of sight, but it is more present. My eyes have also helped me survive. My eyes, in my hardest moments, permitted me to relegate Paul's

73

shoes or his anxious face during his fleeting visits, to a vague half-distance where, thankfully, they were reduced to a simple spectacle.

Liola, sitting next to her Magadan brother, closes her eyes and becomes a woman again. She is no longer preventing someone else from living, but allowing herself to live. In front of the lift, just before we say goodbye, Kostia touches my lips with his. The blood rises to my cheeks, my heart pounds. It hasn't beaten like that for years, except out of sorrow.

Next Christmas, Kostia was in Moscow and I was visiting there. He brought me in his car to see Mother. Mother didn't say a word to him, she simply watched him out of the corner of her eye, a look I knew so well. In fact he was the type of man she would normally have liked, well-dressed, celebrated, a writer. She simply held it against him that he wasn't Paul. That was all. Mother was always the same. She would never ask me how Paul treated me, but how I treated Paul. Father, on the other hand, ended his letters with the question: 'Is Paul still kind to you?'

All of my more unconventional, adventurous acts won my father's support. When I told him about what happened in the 'short trials' which took place in that bastion of Marxist ideology, the Philosophy Faculty, trials officially termed Komsomol Meetings, he listened with great interest. It was Mother who interrupted: 'Not so fast, my little pigeon. Don't stir things up. There is only one thing you have to do and that's keep quiet. You can't defend everyone. One day you'll have to pay for that kind of thing.'

During that first year at university, I took up the defence of a boy called Levy. His only sin was that he invented stories. A mythomaniac. He invented a great love: his wife. He invented a little son: David, aged three. These were his only topic of conversation. He always kept us up to date on his wife's medical check-ups, his son's vaccinations. 'David is in hospital. I'll be able to give you more news of him tomorrow, I'm going to see him tonight.' And we would rush out and buy oranges or a story book with illustrations.

75

Then a Komsomol meeting was announced. The agenda for the day read: 'First, Budapest. Second, The Moral Character of Alexander Levy.'

After Alberto, an Italian communist student of rare intelligence, whom I liked a lot, had shed his light on events in Budapest, the examination of Alexander Levy's moral character was announced. I couldn't sit still. We were about to be 'illuminated' as they used to say.

We were told that the said Alexander Levy had neither wife nor child, that he made use of this imaginary family to skip classes and to sit exams at odd times, in short that he was a corrupt degenerate. The adjective 'capitalist' wasn't used, but it came to the same thing. Alexander Levy stood by the side of the praesidium rostrum. I looked at his red hair, his thin body, his worn grey suit. In the satchel for my books, I had two oranges for his son David: the son who was in hospital; the son who, according to the comrades, didn't exist in reality. One after another the students went up to the rostrum and so abused Alexander Levy that the fact that he had neither wife nor son no longer shocked or surprised me. To invent a wife and a son seemed to me as plausible a way as any other for getting through a life. What did shock me was the students' hatred, the cheapness of their arguments, the filth that they were heaping on Alexander Levy. They were using lies which far surpassed his: and whereas his lie touched me, theirs were disgusting. To destroy the last shreds of Alexander Levy's moral character, the final orator brandished before the dumbfounded public a medical certificate which testified that Levy had gonorrhea. I was furious. Two friends tried to hold me back. They clutched at my skirt. But they couldn't stop me. I arrived at the rostrum, and I made a fateful speech which ensured that during the next five years, I would always risk being accused of every possible subversion. My errors were categorized as those of an 'abstract humanist'.

Only later was I to learn how qualified in

humanism my colleagues were. Krushchev, with all his reformative zeal, had decided to change the security services from top to bottom. He did so, but this meant recycling countless people who lost their jobs. The denunciations, the tortures, the assassinations —there had been so many accomplices, so many jobs! Among these freshly unemployed, some of the young ones, those of thirty or thirty-five, had been judged recuperable by the mother ideology, and a number of them had ended up in the Philosophy Faculty of Moscow University: that same Faculty to which my own thirst for knowledge had drawn me.

On my arrival in this ideological nursery, I was amazed to see so many strange worn-out men, who seemed to me as old as the world. I had no idea who they were. I can still see myself, as if it were only yesterday, at the first Russian Composition exam. On either side, my fellow examinees lent towards me, whispering questions. They knew nothing about grammar or spelling or vocabulary. It was incredible. It was inconceivable that they had come out of secondary schools. So where had they come from?

There were two girls of my own age. I was eighteen. We sat together, surrounded by sixty students of the opposite sex who were twice our age. From the start I took a dislike to these men. I should add that they were dowdy, with grey skin, bags under their eyes, thin hair and unpleasant breath.

Maybe it had not been so easy on the other side of the barricades! When I think of the slenderness, the beauty of Kostia's mother after seventeen years in the Gulag, of the vitality and freshness of my friend Andrei, who, after twenty-seven years spent behind the Urals as an Enemy of the People, now lives in the Bois de Boulogne with his dog and cats, I sense a new and monstrous paradox growing. The enemies of the people, when they are not murdered, fare better than their executioners.

Our policeman-philosophers were certainly in a bad state, but this did not prevent them blustering. Coarsely and lewdly. Afflicted with various ailments—of the liver, stomach, heart, bladder—they ate in the Special Diets Section of the University Cafeteria. Nevertheless, they still had all kinds of short and long-term sexual plans concerning those of us who didn't eat in that cafeteria. Because I refused their propositions, I was undoubtedly granted the honour of being added to their list of Potential Enemies of the People.

I was to pay the price of this later after the rudiments of my Belgian French had led to my encounter with Paul. Paul would come to meet me in the University Hall on Moknovaia Street, just opposite the Kremlin. He used to stroll along the corridor leading to the library. He even used the toilets. This was perfectly understandable since outside it was snowing and freezing. But for our new philosophers and one-time night-watchman of ideology, everything Paul did was suspect. He was prying into the most secret places of the body of socialist construction. He wasn't a member of the French Communist Party, he didn't write for the Communist press. And so he was a spy, disguised as a bourgeois journalist.

And now it was to be my turn for a trial and a warning. Clearly the new philosophers, while leafing through their Hegel or Kant, had remained in touch with the 'special branch' of Lomonossov University, who still had close links with their former organization. And their vengeance bore fruit.

My physical appearance began to alarm Mother. I lost pounds. I was pale. Paul kept leaving and coming back. And if one day he didn't come back? No, Mother protested against herself, that she couldn't believe! Paul was Paul and her little Liola wasn't a young woman to be left in the lurch! I told her nothing of the interrogations which were monthly, then weekly and finally daily. My friends among both students and professors, who knew what was going on behind my back, kept telling me: 'Forget your Frenchman. Here you have a future in front of you, at least a scientific future! As for the rest. . . , you'll manage like we do.' I was determined not to give in. Each morning I got myself an injection and with its help I could endure the cross-examinations, I could argue back, I could even get angry enough to slam the door in their faces.

I was twenty when I loved Paul. Perhaps it was this more than the morning injections which gave me my strength. Fifteen years later when I was again summoning up all my strength, this time to throw Paul out, I was only helping him to realize one of his dreams. Just as, earlier, I had recognized and defended Alexander Levy's right to have a dream: his right to invent a child and a great love for himself, because this made it easier for him to live. Alexander Levy had killed and harmed nobody, and the disappointment I felt at not being able to give two oranges to his son, David, was nothing compared to what he must have suffered before inventing his dream. He was Jewish; I wasn't. He already knew a thousand things about what was going on which I would only learn later. He was more desperate than I, and he had reason to be. And probably he was more honest than I. I hadn't reasoned things out during the Komsomol meeting. None of my actions was very conscious, I was simply carried along by a force which came to me from afar, perhaps the same force which, one day in October fifteen years later, enabled me to pack Paul's bag. Paul, who had a wife and child who weren't imaginary.

It was a very warm autumn. By the window at Gif both the apples from the trees and the night, seemed to be falling together. Plouf! We listened together, Kostia and I, Kostia who was leaving for Moscow the next day. Is there anything better on this earth than recognizing one another in the night, when we are at last ourselves?

The French say: 'Vivre sa vie'. To live one's life. Jean-Luc used the phrase as a title for a film. He knows that it is untrue. We don't live our lives. We are lived by life.

Another Swiss filmmaker, Michel—whom Paul likes and I do too because he is honest and generous—was waiting in his car for his wife Andrienne. Andrienne I think was at the dentist's. Michel is reading the script for a television film he's making. He raises his head and notices Jean-Luc who is standing by a bus stop in the middle of the road; clearly he must be waiting to go to Geneva, whilst Michel is going to Lausanne. So Michel does nothing. He holds Jean-Luc in such esteem that he doesn't want to take him by surprise by tooting and perhaps interrupting a stream of thought. It's a pity, thinks Michel, for he can very well see that Jean-Luc, standing in the sun, is much too hot. It's scarcely the beginning of spring, more like the end of winter, but the heat is oppressive. That morning, Jean-Luc had put on a heavy beige woollen suit—one of those ill-fitting suits he likes so much; he didn't know it was going to be so hot. Michel goes back to reading his script. Five minutes later, he looks up again. Jean-Luc has disappeared. He's taken the bus, Michel thinks, and Andrienne hasn't come yet. He goes on reading for another ten minutes. He looks up again, Jean-Luc is there, standing in exactly the same spot. Only now, he is holding a white bulging plastic bag, and he's wearing a suit of a nondescript grey, made of a nondescript synthetic fabric, even less smart than the previous one, but much lighter. It is a suit absolutely without character, such as only Jean-Luc knows how to find. He must have found it in the super-market opposite. He doesn't move, he is waiting. He is feeling better, less hot. Then through his sun glasses he notices Michel in his car. Michel, a little shy and fascinated by the change of clothes, the lack of fuss, the insousiance of the whole scene, waves to Jean-Luc. Jean-Luc, who now guesses that Michel has followed the whole sequence of events, gives Michel a faint, brief smile, a minimal smile. Then he jumps into the bus which has just drawn up.

This story, which Michel told to Paul and Paul to me, made an impression on me. Partly because I know Jean-Luc's minimal smile and partly because, imagining this scene, I see

Jean-Luc living his life, or rather being obedient to it. A simple change of temperature obliges a stubborn man like Jean-Luc to go through a whole series of actions. He may go through them hurriedly, with his eyes shut, and of course without a thought about how he may appear to others. Nevertheless, the change of temperature obliges him to go through these actions. Life lived Jean-Luc. And Jean-Luc, because he has grace, slipped past his partner, life. Such grace is very rare, a tiny breath of air between two doors, between two words, a tiny light which is almost nothing, and yet a gift. Sometimes, Jean-Luc emits this light, briefly, intimately, like one of his grave, vague smiles.

He and Paul shared something. They could sit opposite one another for hours on end without saying a word. In front of Jean-Luc, Paul felt like a nobody. He didn't tell me this and he didn't suffer from it. Paul has always been too much of a masochist to suffer—on top of everything else—from the failures he invents for himself. They were like two brothers. Now Paul misses Jean-Luc deeply. Yet for ten years, they haven't seen each other. How can I doubt Paul's faculty of forgetfulness?

Mother has turned towards the wall. I can no longer see her hollow cheeks. I see only Xenia turned toward the wall; this was the moment for which Father used to wait so that he could go and take a swig from the bottle of vodka which he had hidden behind the bath.

The Xenia-Vassia couple began with a sack of flour. During the year '28–'29, which our historians no longer refer to as the year of 'Stalin's accession', Mother had already given birth to a son. Her first husband—she used to tell me about him—was odd. He beat her. She had a lot of trouble getting rid of him. Then she found herself alone with her baby in the Ukraine. The Ukraine was also going through a hard time: collectivization and industrialization. At night Mother would barricade her door, because her ex-husband, who had an important job in the local Soviet, was doing everything in his power to try to get her back. At that time Vassia was working in a flour mill and he had taken note of Mother's difficult position. And so, one evening, covered in white flour, a sack over his shoulder, he knocked at her door. The sack meant that Mother and her baby could survive for at least another month.

My Aunt Tanya used to tell me that Father in those days was irresistible, he could seduce anyone he chose even without a sack of flour. He sang. He played the guitar. He didn't drink. When he worked at the mill, he was only nineteen. Mother was twenty-four. They got married straightaway because Father had to leave to do his military service in Kiev.

Today, before coming to the hospital, I spent the day with Aunt Tanya. She is my mother's sister. Tonight she left for the Ukraine, for the house where I was born and where Father delivered his sack of flour. I wanted her to rest and eat before taking the train. I also wanted to see her alone. Soon she

would be the only survivor from my childhood, the last member of my family.

The porter took Aunt Tanya's luggage up
to my room. There was her suitcase with a
strap around it. It seemed to me she had had
this case since the beginning of time. There
were two boxes tied up with cord. There were
string bags in which I could see toilet paper
(this fortnight, thanks to some Plan, there was
shortage throughout the Soviet Union), tins of
Bulgarian food, a salami from the charcuterie
at Gif.

'Now,' I said, 'We're going downstairs.'

'But Liolitchka, I'm not well enough
dressed. Everything's crumpled and anyway,
I'm wearing grey. Let's have something in the
room. No one will see us.'

'You are neither crumpled, nor grey. Come
on.'

I put a pink scarf round her shoulders and
dragged her to the lift. She looked like an
apple, slightly wrinkled, but above all, sun-
drenched. Taking her courage in two hands,
she crossed the hotel lobby full of foreigners.

How these foreigners dress themselves up for their visit to the Homeland of Socialism needs to be seen to be believed! We got to the restaurant. Aunt Tanya had never seen it before, and it was beautiful. A large room under a glass dome, wooden panels, big tables, sculptures, candelabra, white well-starched linen, carpets, fountains, green plants. Two waiters in black jackets rushed forward to welcome us. The room was empty: it was too early, only noon. We were given a big table for two. After a little white wine, my Aunt was completely at her ease. We forgot about Mother, not really, but a little, the weight of the last few days was slightly lifted, we grew younger.

For two months Aunt Tanya had been away from her house in the Ukraine, her house with her two dogs, her cats, her rabbits, her goats, the coal that she puts in the stove each morning. For two months, despite her age, it was she who had been looking after Mother in Moscow. She hadn't wanted me to be told of the gravity of Mother's illness but I came nonetheless. She had been the nurse. Aunt Tanya is like that. She has always assumed and taken responsibility. Her father and mother, my grandparents, both died when she was fourteen. She became the head of the family. Her little sister, my mother, was eight, and her brother, Uncle Vanya, was three. The Imperialist War, as the Russians call the war of 1914; then the Revolution, then the Civil War. It was always a question of finding enough to eat and Aunt Tanya used her wits. With the wood from logs and with old potato sacks, she made shoes which she sold. With this money, she bought tripe and flour and made meat patés which Mother, still a little girl, used to sell in the nearest railway station.

Their house was the one in which I was born. After the war I used to come every year from Moscow to spend the summer there. Its floors smell of freshly washed planks of wood. At night, the sky is very low and black. The windows are open and in the house there is the scent of mint, of roses, of ripe tomatoes. From the house you can hear trains and their whistles. I see myself there, especially from the age of about ten. I washed the floor, I cut up the vegetables for the borscht. At night Uncle Vanya would come home and I would play the fool. There was a neighbour, a young girl, who was dying of tuberculosis. In the evening she came round to our house and I clowned for her. I clowned with all my might, because when she laughed she looked less pale. Besides I knew how real clowns went about it. Thanks to Father I had seen them.

When he came back from the front, Father needed a little amusement. We had left the village in the Urals for the town of Tchkalov, where, despite his wounds, he had to await army orders. Then the Moscow Circus turned up in Tchkalov. I developed a passion for one of the clowns. After the day's work, Father and I would go to the circus. We knew all the acts by heart, and they scarcely interested me any more. It was the life backstage which attracted me. The smell of sawdust and of animals, and my elephant Josef who slept next to the dressing room of our clown. I say 'our' because he was Father's friend as well as mine.

There is still for me something peculiarly dramatic about this backstage life of the circus. There was a man who slashed his wrists for a tightrope walker. There was a dancer who killed herself for love by throwing herself under the feet of her horse. Even the war, in those circus tents, didn't put personal tragedies into perspective. And I, I loved my clown.

'Mother,' I would say, 'I'm going out. I want this scarf, this skirt, this blouse.' Father would take my hand and we would set out on our adventure. Our clown's name was Salomon. Monia for short. He was making up in his dressing room. I watched him. When he began, he was a person like Father; then he was no longer a person at all, but something else. In front of the mirror with the electric light bulbs around it, he dabbed his face with reds, blues, blacks, greens, and while he worked he drank with Father, a mixture of vodka and beer. The two never stopped talking. I no longer remember about what.

93

Now that Father's dead, I wish I could remember. Not even Aunt Tanya can tell me, for at that time she was in the German-occupied Ukraine.

I spent only my holidays with Aunt Tanya, yet after each visit I noticed a change in myself, a growing-up which was more marked than any I noticed after months at school. What was it that was so special about her? Why did she have this power?

When you were with her, the world began to sing, the simplest things became appealing: gathering grass for the rabbits; feeding the ducks at the bottom of the garden; eating the eggs of these ducks. They were gigantic and they were our principal source of protein. The monstrous size of the eggs repelled me, but my Aunt, through a long ritual she invented, made me forget this. For me she was like a good witch, and she ran a kind of chemist's shop. She never bought the medicines which the sick came to get from her; she made them herself. She made aspirin from a fermented sugar which she extracted from willow trees along the Dnieper on certain prescribed days of the year. She always treated herself with her own medicines and they must have agreed with her. She is straight and upright; her hair has kept its beautiful chestnut colour; her skin, though wrinkled, is very fresh; her eyes are brilliant; her voice is firm, and she is seventy-eight. And now, in one of Moscow's most snobbish restaurants, she was a hundred per cent herself. I like people who manage to be themselves in all circumstances, who are at home with whatever is at hand.

In the Zelenograd flat, before Mother was taken to hospital, I had impressed my Aunt with a fish I cooked. I just threw it with some vegetables and herbs, not in the oven. For her there was something comic about this fish, its taste, the fact that it was so easy to cook. And now, in the restaurant, she wanted to eat fish again. The maître d'hôtel was pouring the Tsinandali into the crystal-stemmed glasses. She must have found the ritual and the luxury a little shocking, yet she smiled, and paid little attention to those who were serving us. They, on the contrary, were fascinated by the odd couple we made. Their usual clientele belonged to a smart set of high-ranking officers, of rich Georgians, of political bosses escorting women in heavy make-up and vulgar, extravagant dresses; if it weren't for the nouveau-riche vulgarity of what they wore, some of these women would be beautiful. It is difficult to be a woman in the Soviet Union, even more difficult than in the West.

The usual clientele of the Metropole eat voraciously, drink enough to die of the next day, and dance to the din of a retro orchestra with a fat singer in lamé who howls into a mike. How far away such a Moscow restaurant is from the way ordinary Russians eat! We usually eat in the kitchen, home-made food. And it's there that we talk for hours, relaxed, affectionate. Even in the days of scarcity and terror, there was always a little warm happiness in our kitchens. There was such happiness in my parents' kitchen in the old Kuntsevo flat, where I did my homework on the corner of the polished table. It was the same at my brother's and my schoolfriends'. It is the same today at the flat of my actor friend in Herzen Street. In my own kitchen at Gif, or in Nastia's at Montrouge, or Nekrassov's in Pigalle, we re-create this happiness. Even on the isle of Patmos, in a Greek shipowner's palace in which we were camping, we established a kind of Russian kitchen, where we drank tea and listened to Victor Platonovitch talking.

Aunt Tanya smiled. I had the feeling I was living a decisive moment. Mother was leaving me. Paul had already left. With these two losses I had to go on living, and I had nobody, except for a little while longer, my Aunt Tanya, to help me find the old Liola again. The Liola who had been so good at living, so full of unshakeable hope, the Liola who had been both a fighter and a clown. We were eating the fish and I was looking for this Liola who had become as ghostly as the white flour on Father's shoulders when he came to ask Mother to marry him.

The jig-saw puzzle I was trying to put

97

together was the same one I'd broken into pieces with Paul's complicity. This had happened without either of us being aware of it. I'll never be able to do justice to Paul's innocence. We were, we are, whatever happens, grafted one to another. There is no virtue in this. We both have the same score, a score chalked up by fear. This is why, as I sat there looking at my Aunt, I was perhaps too bruised, too lost.

'A little more?' I poured some Tsinandali into my Aunt's wine glass. We were talking of simple truths. 'You drink wine, you eat fish, you are alive, your blood is being pumped through your body, you are not losing blood. In that case one is lucky, don't you think so Auntie?'

'No!' Aunt Tanya disagreed with my definition of luck. She was looking at me oddly, a little obliquely. It didn't seem right to her that I, who was so young and so successful (this was the word she and Mother used when talking about me), it didn't seem right to her that I should continually define Life by its negative complement which is Death. Death was at Mother's door, not mine. I was going to stay. Aunt Tanya was no longer on my side, and for once she didn't know how to react. She didn't want to follow me; I was frightening her.

One night long ago, in the very same restaurant of the Metropole, I danced with Paul. It wasn't easy. We were trying to match our steps in a way which would go on for years and years. The next day Paul was leaving for Paris. We weren't married yet. While dancing, I was doing my utmost to make my illusions true. Paul has the capacity to switch on people's illusions: he's a lamplighter, like Fenosa's grandfather. He walks on, he wanders around and he forgets to put out his lamps. 'But why are they alight?' he asks. 'I couldn't have done that, I'm not that clever.' At each step he is totally innocent. The more lamps he lights, the more he forgets and becomes modest.

I wiped out this memory of dancing in the same restaurant and said whatever came into

my head, so as to dispel the sadness I was beginning to communicate to my Aunt. I talked
without thinking about the tomatoes which
grow crazily on the balcony of my bedroom
at Gif, about the flowers Paul buys for Pauline
and me, about other presents. We sounded a
perfect family. I said nothing about chucking
Paul out.

Regularly and stubbornly I repeated to
Paul, 'If only you would not come back to the
house any more, you wouldn't have to leave.'
It seemed so simple to me. I always tried to
communicate with Paul in simple words. But
they fell into a void.

When Paul stopped sleeping in the house,
I didn't want to see any more the bed which
he had bought before my arrival in France.
With the help of a neighbour, Paul carried
the bed down to the cellar. 'First they kick
the man out of the door; then they throw
out the mattress!' He said this in a
very gentlemanly fashion and we all three
laughed.

In Aunt Tanya's house there were bookshelves. By the age of nine, I knew what happened when a beautiful noblewoman had an assignation at night with her gamekeeper in an arbour on the edge of a precipice! I flipped through the pages of the yellow magazine, *Niva*, which dated from before the Revolution. There, for the first time, I saw engraved in black ink the body of a naked young woman. It was moving, even more so because the scene was a morgue: the reader discovered the body at the same time as the doctor who was just lifting the sheet. Every summer I went back to this engraving which so fascinated me, and every summer my own growing body resembled a little more that of the dead woman's: the same forms, the same lines. She could only just have died, for she seemed so alive lying there on the table. And the doctor's gesture was so pathetic. In the Soviet Union there are no statues in public squares of nude women. On Aunt Tanya's bookshelves there were also poems by Tioutchev, a writer who is not mentioned in our school books. 'I remember those times, those golden

101

times, and everything in me grows hot.' 'In these late days of the year, a moment comes when something gasps in us like the breath of spring.' In Tioutchev's rather bad poems my ten-year-old heart found an assurance, a guarantee of permanence. They didn't make me dream, they gave me strength. I remembered this strength now and wanted to ask my Aunt about her house and the spring and the summer. But we had no time, and we couldn't afford to miss the train. I had to see my Aunt off properly. I fetched her luggage, found a taxi, put the carrier bags on her seat, arranged the suitcases in the luggage rack, and then went to get her some oranges. She couldn't leave for her small town without oranges, which are one of the principal sources of Vitamin C in winter. Whole families were asleep on the benches in the station. There was a lot of marble, and in a large baroque buffet, there were sausages and gherkins, but there were no oranges. I write the word 'oranges' and I'm finished. I can't go on.

Pistol shots can sometimes save your life. We've seen that. Thanks to the pistol shots, my body, ready for the morgue, found its oxygen. In the Botkin hospital I had to stay in a little room for what seemed, to a three-year-old, an eternity. An entire wall of this room, giving on to the hall, was made of glass. The nurses could watch me without having to come in. My illness was thought to be infectious and I was not allowed any visitors. But on my left there was a window, behind which, several times a day, Father appeared. Through the window I watched him perform all the tricks he had learnt from our clown. Once he brought a prop with him, it was an orange. He had nothing else in his pockets. I couldn't hear what he said through the thick glass. With just the orange, he acted out a whole play, and behind him was a backdrop of snow, frozen trees and blue sky. That same morning I had undergone a serious operation without anaesthetic. Two strong male nurses had held my arms and legs while an abscess on my bottom, caused by the injections I had been hurriedly given on arrival, was lanced. I was devastated, not because of the pain the scalpel caused me, but because of the nurses' violence. I had never before experienced violence. The orange Father was playing with made me forget it all.

I return to the beach in Catalonia. I am swimming and then I come out of the sea and I notice one of Franco's policemen in uniform, dragging a dog along with a hideous instrument. It's a stick, long, thick, rigid. At the end there's a large chain. The instrument permits the dog to be caught and then be held at a distance while he's dragged towards the pound vehicle. The dog undergoes torture. He can't breathe. He is struggling and can barely yelp. His eyes look mad. Shocked, the bathers have formed a little crowd. I run towards them, I no longer recognize myself, everything happens as if I weren't myself but someone else, I am far away, I can no longer see the dog, only the two male nurses who hold my arms and legs. I see the dog suffering agony behind some steel bars and myself on the other side of the bars, I am juggling with two oranges, but the dog doesn't see me, he is bounding away. I am holding the large stick, trying to tear it away. I can't. I hit the policeman, bite his fists. He lets go of the stick and I run towards the car with the dog, who does not resist but pulls me along.

An hour later a Civil Guard came to the front door of Fenosa's house—where I was staying. I made out certain words in Catalan: prison, insult to authority, foreigner. In this part of Catalonia, Fenosa is a sage, a kind of national monument. And so I was excused on the understanding that I left the next morning with the dog.

Mother turns towards me, but without seeing me, for she's asleep. It was she who used to watch over me when I was ill. I never knew any violence at home, not even verbal. Not even when I came home after having spent my first night with a man, although Father didn't like it.

I came home around five o'clock on the first morning train. That gave me two hours in which to recuperate a little before leaving again for the Lenin Library. I couldn't sleep. The eiderdown pulled up to my eyes, I listened to Xenia's and Vassia's muffled voices coming from the kitchen. Every morning Father ate cabbage soup. Mother watched him eat, then helped him get dressed. She put his watch on his wrist, she laced his shoes and she strapped on his arm. That morning they talked of me, trying to come to terms with the unprecedented event of my sleeping out. Father spoke loudest, but he did not shout. All this, he said, was Mother's fault! She answered him quietly: 'Liola is serious. She knows what she's doing.' Their habitual roles were reversed. Mother was the one who was always reprimanding me for little things, Father the one who defended me. 'Serious, serious!' Father growled, 'She knows nothing about life . . . She'll be hurt . . . '

But to me nothing was said, no reproach made. When Father kissed me before going off to work, I could feel how that morning he made a special effort not to hug me harder

106

than usual. The tiny breath of grace, the tiny breath between two words . . .

After Father's death I wrote a rambling letter to Mother in which I reminded her, among other things, of that kitchen where they both spoke in low voices after my first night spent away from home. I thanked them for being parents like that. Father died in the street while getting off a bus: Bus number 7, Kiev Station-Kuntsevo, the bus that Paul and I liked because it went by a little forest and stopped in front of wooden dashas. Stretched out in the snow, Father held in his only hand a string bag containing a large packet of buckwheat for making kasha, and a bouquet of mimosa. It was March 8th, Women's Day.

By the mere fact that he no longer sleeps with me, Paul makes me rediscover so much of my past. Including that night with Iouri, my first night spent with a man. I hadn't thought of it for years, yet now it comes back to me vividly. It happened twenty years ago when I was slowly recovering from my first unhappy love affair, a platonic one. 'Always unhappy,' said Father, to whom I told everything. 'First love affairs are always unhappy. It's normal comrade, quite normal.' We had these conversations together, and we used to call them 'Talking about Life', as if it were the title of a radio programme. These conversations took place on one condition: Mother's absence. This condition guaranteed the second, which was the supply of vodka. We sat facing each other in the kitchen, Father poured himself little glasses, and I drank tea. So far as I was concerned, Mother was wrong about only one thing. Right up to the end she scolded Father, if she so much as saw a glass in his hand. I told her this, but there was nothing to be done.

As soon as Father came back from the front, I understood once and for all that he needed vodka and he needed the company that goes with drinking it: the company of the clown Salomon, or my own, or even the company of another woman. Mother, who was a fury to any of her rivals, certainly did not share this view. I once saw her break an umbrella over the head of a woman who had shown herself

108

susceptible to Father's wooden arm and his new 'Tsarist' uniform made from the finest wool. As for me, I wasn't frightened. I was sure that Father, one-armed philanderer that he may have been, would never leave us. Just as I was sure that Paul, when he began to be haunted, would never leave me.

Paul did not have the same sort of confidence when I told him that I was intrigued by an English author whom I had met at a friend's dinner—Paul never went out with me in the evening, for he had a horror of social occasions. He immediately started to hate everything English, and it was this that led him to his studies of Joan of Arc. He grew thin, he suffered from vertigo and pains in the heart, he started to drink Extra Dry Gin straight from the bottle.

I didn't know what to do to reassure him, I repainted the bedroom in pale pink, I wrote a novel for him in which a real enemy, a formidable one, the KGB, separated a man and a woman who resembled us a little.

I learnt my lesson: there is nothing worse than making those who are attached to you suffer. With my pink walls, my novel, I tried to tell Paul that we were inseparable. He looked at the room, he read the book and, as if he felt nothing, he simply said: 'It's beautiful. I don't know how you do it. It's really beautiful.' I was desperate. I hadn't left Paul. I had dreamed of my Englishman for a fortnight and then one morning I coldly drew a line through that dream, because I loved Paul. Five years later, Paul was to tell me, while putting his shoes back on: 'Everyone separates; everyone lives like that nowadays.'

The Lenin Library in Moscow doesn't close until ten in the evening. For me this is a sign of civilization. I was working on the ground floor, between two bookcases full of old books with green and gold bindings, next to a window which looked out onto the park—I had this special place as a favour from the very pretty woman librarian, who also made sure that I was not disturbed by the propositions of that strange race of bustling sex-starved men who, pursuing their mysterious occupations, haunt, as they do elsewhere, the public libraries of Russia. It was the beginning of term. Sun-tanned from Aunt Tanya's Scythian sun, I was all ready to throw myself into my course of German philosophy.

At ten on the September evening in question, I was queuing up to return a pile of books, my head a little dazed by what I had read about the Master-Slave dialectic. Suddenly I felt a pair of eyes on me. There are times when you feel a look as if it were heat or light, something altogether physical. And I felt this look at a very precise spot: where my neck meets my back.

I turn around. I see a figure dressed in beige, blond, a man. He doesn't smile. Nor do I. His eyes are grave. I am tired, or rather, hungry. I am thinking of the tomato juice I will drink in three minutes time at the Lenin Library tube station. I drink one there every evening, it stops me feeling hungry. He follows me to the exit and I am surprised to find myself not walking towards the station but beside him,

111

although he hasn't yet said a word. I keep pace with him, as if we were both subject to the same tropism, and at the same time, I discover a whole new district, a part of Moscow I didn't know. Every morning I pass by here, but I have never before ventured into these streets. A mistake, I tell myself, because I like these courtyards with trees and wooden benches, and the walls of the houses painted ochre, rose, indigo, and their double windows full of jamjars, cats, flowers.

Without a word, we walk a long way, perhaps three kilometres. We stop by a theatre which I recognize. In rather bedraggled costumes they perform plays by Lope de Vega. My friend, Iriana Pushkin, had a passion for this theatre and sometimes we went together. The door which my companion opens for me is just beside the theatre. We climb the stairs. The paint is peeling, and you can see all the colours that previously covered the wall: pink, white, green. The staircase is of old wood whose knots and grains look alive. I have never

112

before seen such a staircase. I will see others, years later, on the Left Bank in Paris.

Now I'm out of my element, and in a moment I'll be even more so when we go into a large well-proportioned room where there are bare beams, a fireplace, a large bed covered with a patchwork quilt and, in front of it, a wooden country bench. The young man turns every light on one by one, and disappears. Everything is new to me here. I pass my hand over the patchwork quilt and I tell myself out loud, that it is here and nowhere else that I shall lose my virginity. I have an account to settle with this virginity. For over a year it has made me feel like an invalid.

He was tall I think, with something slightly feminine about him, perhaps as a result of his blond hair; he had a long face which made him look serious. He seemed so inexperienced that I felt confident. In a glass on the bench in front of me were two white gladioli with short stems. I don't like gladioli, but these two looked very beautiful. And everything else too, the silence of the room, the gestures with

113

which Iouri poured out the Hungarian wine, gliding graceful gestures.

Silently we drink and the wine makes me hungry. Without my saying anything, he gets up and brings back bread, butter, cheese. He cuts the cheese and I notice his long fingers. He does everything nonchalantly, as if it had nothing to do with him. Again he disappears, and comes back with two hardboiled eggs. I can't eat these eggs, but they win me over completely: the final gesture of the first Act in his theatre of silence. In order to survive, one has to forget . . . Yet this doesn't prevent me from recalling and remembering intensely those eggs I never touched.

I got to know only a little about him, except the gentleness, both affectionate and sure, of all his gestures when he understood that it was the first time for me. He told me that his mother was an actress, and that he was finishing his studies at the Literary Institute. He accompanied me to the station on foot. I said I had no telephone, which was true. He gave me his number and I wrote it down with

114

a pencil. 'I'll call you,' I told him, knowing that I never would.

Ten months later I met Paul at Ostankino. And I became his wife. I woke up beside him thousands of times. He would make me black coffee; he would come in and go out of the bedroom, his face covered in shaving soap; he would lean against the radiator and tell me, in his special way, what was going on in the world. He had the gift of making me laugh. In his views, he was like no one else. Each in our solitude, we lived side by side. By this I mean that we shared a great deal without this sharing becoming heavy, without ever swallowing each other up, without having the impression that we owed each other anything. When Paul was anxious, I never reproached him. I let the mood pass, and stayed there by his side. Paul called this 'a certain quality of absence'. I was simply trying to give him my confidence, my optimism. I have this optimism because I grew up in a country unlike other countries, and I grew up between Vassia and Xenia who knew so well how to love me.

115

I too, of course, was capable of being suspicious. Women, including some very beautiful ones, had their eyes on Paul, and it turned out that all the women he had loved before me were equally striking.

Occasionally I was frightened. I say occasionally, because the fear came and went and I never dwelt on it. Paul's presence was made as if to my measure. I didn't want any more. More would have bothered me, prevented me from living my life. Paul and I had an understanding which lasted, and which nothing and nobody will ever be able to efface. We were lucky. Yet a day of reckoning can come.

The first step taken towards that day was mine. I had made Paul ill: an equilibrium had been destroyed. I believe in necessities, in facts which you can't get round, in cycles. Why, for example, after that first night with Iouri which could not have been better, did I know it would never be repeated? Convinced that he would try to see me again, I no longer went to the Lenin Library but registered at the University Library instead.

116

Months passed. There were endless essays to write and exams to take. I put Iouri out of my mind and threw myself into the winter syllabus; then one day I went back to the Lenin Library. It must have been close to the new year, because I can see myself in the smoking room with my friend Iriana and we were talking about New Year's Eve. I didn't see Iouri come in. He was still blond and beige, calm and quiet. He came up to me and he slapped my face. I felt his blow like a rape and I was filled with rage. Just as twenty years later, I was to feel raped by Paul telling me about how he was haunted.

I still carry with me Iouri's mystery and the violence of his gesture which was so unlike the gentleness of our night together. I am still grateful to him. I prolong the night we spent together by musing, by writing novels. To everybody, his method. My own way of living my part, of coming to terms with my destiny, of shaping my days a little, is to write.

In one of the issues of *Continent*, Volodia

Bukovsky talks of the *château* which never left him during his imprisonment. Thrown into solitary confinement, he began to put his *château* in order. In his mind's eye, he planned everything down to the smallest architectural detail, the volutes of the entrance gate, the drawing room fireplace. For a long while he could not bring himself to accept that certain trees in the park of the *château* had grown too old and would have to be cut down; then he hesitated over what trees he should plant in their place.

A KGB officer calls him in for a re-education session and Volodia, while letting the officer talk, puts the finishing touches to a large reception he is holding in his *château*. The oak logs are burning; he slowly opens the heavy carved doors and his friends come in. Which of his wines should he serve first?

I read this, dumbfounded by Bukovsky's prodigious gift for survival, by the marvellous absurdity of his resistance. I believe more and more strongly in the boon of fiction, on paper or in the mind.

118

Once I had a dog staying with me, more a ball of fur than a dog. She was called Kitty, and she belonged to a Russian Jewish family who were scattered all over the world. Kitty ate only one thing: leeks. In the market at Gif I bought a bundle of leeks for her. I also bought carrots, whiting, mandarins. I knew whom I was shopping for and so it was easy: for Kitty and for the friends whom I had invited to dinner. I could already see their faces round the table. Often I watch my friends eating and forget to eat myself. Mother used to do the same.

A few months before I left Russia, I was sent as a future professor of philosophy to lecture about questions of nutrition (in the light of recent Party decisions) to collective farm-workers. This was at the height of the Maize and Khrushchev epoch, when the Party was promising that we would easily overtake American dairy and meat production. In a church, long since transformed into a cultural club, I found myself before my audience, almost all of them women. I couldn't bring

119

out a single word about the radiant meat and milk perspectives which stretched before them. I didn't have the courage, and in any case, they didn't want to listen. They had come to speak, I could feel it. I asked them to do so. First subject: men—there weren't any, this was hard, it meant that they, the women, had to do all the heavy work. Second subject: men, the few who were there drank from morning til night, at sowing time, at harvest time and between times.

One of the women invited me to sleep in her home. She prepared a meal of, as we say in Russia, 'that which God has sent us'. Sixty years after the Great October Revolution, God had sent four boiled potatoes, a sour cabbage and a strip of fatty bacon. Each time I go to the market at Gif and see all the bulging shopping bags, I see them through the eyes of my Russian woman on the collective farm. And I can't get over it, it's like a fairy tale.

Following Paul's departure, there was a period of ten to twelve weeks when any display of food horrified me. Pauline was growing, she needed to eat, but it was hard for me to buy her a cutlet. My woman from the collective farm couldn't help me. The poet Ossip Emilievitch who died in a camp couldn't help me, although he is a poet for whom I have almost the same feelings as for Xenia and Vassia. Ossip is my spiritual Vassia, and he used to ransack the camp rubbish bins searching for something to eat.

The beauty of leeks or cauliflowers meant nothing to me. Only oranges spoke to my heart, and when they did, my heart tightened. Was Paul any more real than the son of Alexander Levy? I imagined Pauline with two oranges in her satchel for Paul. Then I ran home and took a spoonful of Valerian syrup.

The blood plasma bottle is empty. Mother is still asleep, she does not move. Through the curtains, the sky is becoming blue. Perhaps death doesn't exist; perhaps it isn't sad. What is sad is to fall asleep when you have made ready for death and then wake up again. You're back in their clutches and they're

121

incapable of doing anything to make the world they've dragged you back to less fearful, and at the same time they are convinced they've done their duty. I'm not brave enough to want to see Mother wake up again. And anyway, I won't look right for her. It's very hot in the room but I have started shivering. It is time this night ended. I would like to see people waiting for a bus. I would like to see a village in the forest with its chimneys smoking. If things weren't like they are with Paul, my first impulse would be to go to the post office and send him an interminable telegram, one of those telegrams which say nothing, but which used to do Paul and me so much good. But I no longer know how to say nothing to Paul. I am growing more and more cold. I had better begin to tell myself a story. It happens that sometimes I come across Pauline sitting very straight in a chair, not moving, silent, her eyes fixed. 'What on earth are you doing?' I ask her. 'Shush!' she answers, 'I'm telling myself a story.'

In the flat in Zelenograd I read a story by

122

Andrei Platonov—the story of Nikita. The son of a carpenter and a carpenter himself, Nikita comes back to his village at the end of the Civil War. He's still young, his mother is dead, his father is still alive, but his strength is failing. On the road, Nikita meets Liouba whom he knew as a little girl when they both went to school. Liouba's mother, who was a schoolteacher, is dead too. Nikita remembers her house, his father sometimes went there to repair some pieces of furniture. All their fine furniture was sold. Liouba has changed a lot, she's studying medicine in the local town and she reads heavy scholarly books. Nikita sees how she reads these books by the firelight from the half-open stove, how she has a thin neck and pointed knees, how she never eats enough. From the factory canteen where he works, he brings her boiled fish, kasha, bread. He also gathers wood for her stove. The spring comes. Liouba is still reading and Nikita doesn't know what to say to her; she, the cleverer one, tells him that he should marry. He marries her.

The old father's strength comes back to him. He makes them a bed, a wardrobe, but above all he concentrates on making a cot, a child's table, a child's chair. The seasons come and go. Nikita is not able to do to Liouba what a man does to his wife. Liouba is patient and still full of hope. But for Nikita, life has become a nightmare. Platonov doesn't say that he has a nervous breakdown, that's not Platonov's style, but it's like that. Throwing himself into the river would have been a happy end for Nikita.

He doesn't throw himself into the river. Instead he follows a beggar out of the village, ends up in the local town and there gets a job as a cleaner in the market. He no longer speaks at all, people believe that he is deaf and dumb and leave him alone. One day he encounters his father who has come to buy some tools. 'Liouba?' Nikita asks, pronouncing his first word for months. Liouba, his father tells him, threw herself into the river, was fished out, and now she spits blood. The father brings his son back to the village. And now, on the very first night, Nikita makes love to his wife. But this does not stop Liouba from spitting blood. When Platonov wrote his story, there were no antibiotics.

I have no watch. I forgot my cigarettes downstairs in the cloakroom. I now dread waking Mother up.

A man in a white coat has opened the door: it is Vladimir Petrovitch who, this morning, told me what Mother's tumour looks like by showing me his clenched fist.

I get up and follow him into the hall with its green linoleum and shining white walls. We go into a room less heated than Mother's. There is an open window. The atmosphere is smoky. My head is turning a little. As if through a fog, I notice a bad reproduction of a Matisse, a little desk cluttered with papers, a steaming electric kettle, two glasses and a bottle of whiskey—the one I gave to Vladimir Petrovitch this morning. On a little table a lamp, covered with white muslin, gives off a soft light. The Russians have this habit of enveloping lamps in cloths or shawls.

125

Vladimir Petrovitch pushes a chair towards me and himself sits sideways on another. He takes a rather battered packet of cigarettes out of his pocket. Small Smoke, they're called. I recognize them. They're the Moscow equivalent of Gauloises and not bad. I try to recall the title of that painting by Matisse. Silence of a house? The house where silence lives? The silence of an inhabited house? Vladimir Petrovitch pours me out some very strong tea and hands me a cigarette and some matches, without formality, as if to another man.

'What time is it?'

'Six-thirty,' he answers.

'Yesterday you told me about a patient whom you were staying the night for. How is he?'

'He died. Twenty minutes ago,' Vladimir Petrovitch says this in the strictly professional tone I have already heard him use. He opens the whiskey bottle and pours some into his tea.

'Would you like some?'

'No. It won't do you any good either, drinking like this at dawn.'

'This morning, nothing does me any good.'

He is certainly younger than I. One gets worn out more quickly in this country. His hair hasn't been cut in Paris, but in one of a thousand barber shops where they shear your whole head in one fell swoop, with no scruples. He is very tall, very stooped, his eyes are bloodshot, his shirt stained.

'How long do you think Mother can hold out?'

'A month at the most. At her stage, there isn't usually far to go, but the old are sometimes surprising.' He pours himself some more whiskey, and, as if absent-mindedly, pours some into my tea as well.

'There's a lot of dying in your ward?'

'That's all there is. It's the corridor of the condemned. This morning I opened up one of them and closed him up again immediately. I killed him, if you like. Thirty-eight years old. A painter. A friend of mine. There was nothing left to do. Two lungs gone, the trachea. You are from Paris?'

'No, it's my daughter who is from Paris.'

'How old is she?'

'Eleven.'

'After I saw you this morning, I told Pavlik, I've met a Parisian woman.'

Vladimir Petrovitch rummages through his papers and finds what he is looking for.

'Look. This is his last gouache, the painter's. What's your first name?'

'Liola.'

'Like my grandmother.' He smiled, just a little.

'Smiling suits you,' I said, looking at the gouache.

The painting is of a staircase. Somehow the way it is drawn emphasizes its steepness. The staircase stops dead and the light, visible on the wall beside it, makes one feel that the air is foul, unbreathable. I push this image away from me and resent it.

'No, don't cry. One shouldn't cry.'

'Was I crying?' I wasn't aware of it.

128

'Ah yes,' Vladimir Petrovitch says, he isn't a liar and to prove it he passes a finger under my eyes with a medical gesture. Suddenly everything snaps in me, falls apart, starts to tremble. Vladimir Petrovitch picks me up, puts me on his lap and presses my head against his shoulder. How long am I there, my arms around his neck? I don't know, time enough to calm down and to rediscover the courage necessary to return to Mother in her room. They must have increased the dose of her drugs, she's more absent than ever and doesn't speak at all.

It appears that on waking, she made signs to have the flowers taken away from her bedside, I don't tell her that I'm leaving, that my visa expires tonight, that Pauline is expecting me in Paris this evening. I say to myself, 'You are looking at your mother and you are looking at her for the last time.' In the corridor outside, one of the women who shares Mother's room comes up to me and tries to comfort me. She's kind, courageous. I look at her, remembering Vladimir Petrovitch's phrase: the corridor of

129

the condemned. I embrace her, wish her a good recovery and go downstairs.

Kostia is waiting below. The entrance hall is empty. In the cloakroom, a large lady in a white blouse grumbles at me, in fact scolds me, because the little loop on the inside of my coat collar is unsewn; she couldn't hang my coat up on the peg, she says. Her sharp abuse shakes me up and brings me back to life. Ever since I was little, I've been told off by cloakroom attendants, in the Lenin Library, in the opera, in cafés, everywhere, always because the little loop on my coat collar has been missing or unsewn. I smile. A little more and I'll be laughing outright. The attendant calms down. She thinks perhaps I'm mad.

Driving in Kostia's car, I notice for the first time the colossal statue of Lenin standing on the Zelenograd central square. I hadn't noticed before, there were other things on my mind. It is so large and its pedestal is so high that even if you knew it was there, you'd have to screw your neck and deliberately look up to see it. At the same time I see, on a nearby roof, some large neon letters which spell out: 'A newspaper not only makes propaganda for the masses, it activates them.' Signed Lenin.

'You have understood,' says Kostia, 'not only buggers you up with propaganda, but activates you as well. How right they are to insist upon that! We run about, we get bored, we drink, we kick the bucket, and we would be quite capable of forgetting what a newspaper really does. You might just remember that a newspaper buggers the masses with propaganda, but that isn't all! Then you lift up your head to see what the weather looks like, and what you've forgotten comes back to you: A newspaper fucks the masses into activity!'

Kostia is wearing his steel-rimmed spectacles, which we bought together on the Boulevard des Italiens. They are the sort of glasses that nineteenth century revolutionaries wore. He drives perfectly well, but on the road back to Moscow we are stopped three times.

When the police stop a car, the driver is obliged to get out to show his papers. They don't look at the papers, they simply sniff the driver's breath. It's a control without any violence involved, but it's boorish and insulting.

'Can't one protest?'

'It would do no good,' says Kostia, 'but, of course, they'd do better to stop that lorry there!'

I screw up my short-sighted eyes to see the lorry better. A marvel. Huge, broken down, patched up, as if home-made from old wardrobes and plumbing, and on top of this lorry a large wooden chest tied with a rope whose end is whirling round in the air like a lasso, and the lorry is going at top speed, charging along the icy road, in fact, it's not charging, it is flying, it is dancing like death. It spins round, it slips sideways, it continues on the wrong side of the road. Kostia hasn't slowed down, he too is charging after this mad lorry. I start to scream. I no longer know where I am, there is an avalanche of icicles,

132

sunflowers, tombstones, saucers, oranges. 'Kostia,' I scream, 'I'm frightened! Overtake him, overtake him.'

My screams wake me up. Is it that I still want to live?

Isabelle

A Story in Shots

John Berger and Nella Bielski

We would like to thank Hugh Brody, with whom we watched many night skies during the writing of this story.

N.B. and J.B.

Women and Men in the Story

ISABELLE EBERHARDT, a young woman of Russian nationality, born in Geneva

ALEXANDER TROPHIMOWSKI, called 'Vava'; Isabelle's father

NATHALIE EBERHARDT, formerly wife of the Russian general Count Rostovski; Isabelle's mother. She lives with Vava.

AUGUSTIN ROSTOVSKI, sometimes called 'Tiny', son of Nathalie Eberhardt and General Rostovski, Isabelle's half-brother.

DIMA ROSTOVSKI, nicknamed 'Cactophil'; another half-brother of Isabelle

VERA, a Russian medical student studying in Geneva

LELLA HADRA, an Algerian fortune-teller and peddler

JENNY, Augustin Rostovski's French wife

HÉLÈNE, daughter of Augustin and Jenny; Isabelle's niece

LOUIS HUBERT GONZALVE LYAUTEY, colonel, later general in the French army. First stationed in South-East Asia, he becomes the leading figure in the French conquest of Morocco

EUGÈNE LETORD, an officer on the staff of Lyautey

CAPTAIN FRIOUX, a young officer in the Arab Bureau (Intelligence) of the French army in Algeria

SIDI LACHMI, a sherif of the Quadrya Brotherhood, a religious organization involved in resistance against the French

SLIMAN EHNNI, a sergeant of the Spahis, a contingent of Algerian troops that is part of the French army; Isabelle's husband

CAPTAIN JUNOT, an elderly officer in the Arab Bureau

Act 1

WADI BESIDE AIN SEFRA – ALGERIA – OCTOBER 1904

It is hot, the light is brilliant. A French general is standing among a group of functionaries – some officers, some civilians, journalists, perhaps some local dignitaries. The general's name is Louis Hubert Gonzalve Lyautey.

The wadi is wet and small streams of water are disappearing in the hot sand. Baskets, bundles of clothes and pieces of furniture clutter the foreground. French Legionnaires are searching the desert; they are evenly spaced and move in one direction. Officers direct proceedings. The Legionnaires are picking up scraps from the sand and mud.

> LYAUTEY: I gave them an order to search everywhere, every square metre of sand. They are finding scraps of paper, torn pages. One must always think of posterity.

From a small pile that has been assembled by the legionnaires, the French general picks up a notebook and a muddy revolver. The horizon is barely noticeable, sand and sky blend together.

> LYAUTEY: Otherwise no one will remember us.

LAKESIDE – GENEVA – MORNING, FEBRUARY 1886

The lake of Geneva divides the city in half. On the north side there are small harbours. Due to the exceptional cold, these are partly frozen over. Isabelle, nine years old, is with her half-brother Dima, in his mid teens. She has ventured out onto the thin ice. Gulls circle around her.

Dima, standing on the shore, is trying to persuade her to come back. A few passersby along the promenade glance towards the children.

> DIMA: Isabelle, you're walking on very thin ice! Isabelle, come back!

ISABELLE:	It doesn't crack, Cactophil, if you go fast enough!
DIMA:	You're going to drown, Isabelle!
ISABELLE:	It's my birthday and I want to go to the other side.
DIMA:	Come back, Is–a–belle!

Dima is joined by a Park Attendant and a Policeman. The Policeman shouts to Isabelle through a megaphone.

She is a hundred or so yards away. A small crowd has gathered.

POLICEMAN:	It is strictly forbidden to walk on the ice where you are . . . Can you hear me . . . It is forbidden!

Isabelle waves, as if hearing applause, and continues. Meanwhile, Vava, Isabelle's father, a large, black-bearded man in his late forties, has arrived at the shore. He seizes the megaphone and speaks in a strong Russian accent.

VAVA:	Diogenes, my daughter . . . can you hear me? Today you are nine, Diogenes, and your life is before you. You haven't learnt enough . . . come back to us.

For a moment Isabelle is absolutely stationary. Then she carefully picks her way back towards the quayside and the waiting crowd.

POLICE STATION – GENEVA

Behind the counter, a Swiss Police Officer is seated at a table, and a Second Officer is standing by a filing cabinet. Vava gives the impression that the chair on which he is sitting is too small for him. Isabelle and Dima are seated side by side on a bench against the wall. They stare aggressively at the policemen.

FIRST OFFICER:	She is your daughter?
VAVA:	Correct.
FIRST OFFICER:	Why was she not in school this morning?

VAVA: She does not go to school.

FIRST OFFICER: Education is compulsory.

VAVA: I don't believe in your education of half-truths. I teach her at home.

The Second Officer pulls a file out of his cabinet, and moves in the direction of the First Officer.

FIRST OFFICER: Can she read and write?

VAVA: You were thinking of which language, Superintendent?

FIRST OFFICER: I'm asking if she can write.

VAVA: In Arabic, in French, in Russian, in Greek – she can write.

FIRST OFFICER: Mr Trophimowski, up to now I and my colleague have been patient . . .

VAVA: Diogenes, write your name for our servant of the people!

She writes in Latin: Isabelle. Then she adds her name below, in Arabic letters.

The Second Officer puts the opened file on the desk in front of the First Officer, who glances at the cover.

SECOND OFFICER: Another one!

FIRST OFFICER: Mad Russians, more every year!

The Second Officer runs through the file while showing it to the First Officer. They are both bent over the desk.

SECOND OFFICER: Alexander Trophimowski, former priest of Russian church . . . member of the World Anarchist Association since 1868 . . . family tutor to the children of General Count Rostovski . . . absconded with General's wife, Nathalie Eberhardt, and her two sons . . . applied for political asylum in the Canton of Geneva in 1875 . . .

Isabelle goes over to her father, sits on his knee, plays with his beard. The Second Officer raises his voice.

SECOND OFFICER:	. . . uses money obtained from concubine's husband, the aforementioned General Rostovski, to buy Villa Nuova in the village of Meyrin . . . illegitimate daughter born in Cantonal Hospital 1877 . . .
FIRST OFFICER:	Listed, since several years, as politically harmless.

GARDEN OF VILLA NUOVA – MEYRIN – AFTERNOON, MAY 1897

The Villa Nuova is a large, neglected, nineteenth-century house. The leaves of unkempt rhododendron bushes glisten in the afternoon sun. In a broken-down summer house, a woman is giggling.

The woman slips furtively away from the pavilion to disappear between the trees. Isabelle, in boots, trousers, and with a spade on her shoulder, walks slowly down the path. She walks like a man. The pavilion has a domed roof, and windows all the way around. Some are broken. A man, dandyish, blue eyes, tall, appears in the doorway. He is Augustin, Isabelle's half-brother.

ISABELLE:	You've just fucked her.
AUGUSTIN:	You and your foul mouth!
ISABELLE:	You and your chicken-brained flirtations. You make me sick, Augustin.
AUGUSTIN:	You're jealous, that's all, jealous! And how vulgar it is for a sister to be jealous of her brother.
ISABELLE:	Half-brother! I adore it when you play the aristocrat. My Tiny who can't forget he's Count Rostovski!

Isabelle sits down on a bench. She lights a cigarette. Enter Dima, carrying a large cactus and wearing the same clothes as his brother and half-sister. These clothes on the three of them look like Russian peasant uniforms. Dima addresses Augustin and Isabelle, who do not look at him.

144

DIMA: As usual, Brother Augustin and Sister Isabelle
          are discussing their feelings.

Dima pulls out a notebook with a pencil attached, and reads from it.

DIMA: There are cabbages to thin and plant, pea stalks
          to gather and cut, tomato plants to water, and
          the trout pond to be cleaned. An order to pay
          934 francs has just been delivered by a bailiff.
          One shouldn't play cards if one is not lucky at
          them, Augustin.

An elderly lady comes slowly towards the pavilion, untidily
dressed but in clothes that were once elegant. This is Nathalie,
mother of Dima, Augustin, and Isabelle.

NATHALIE: Dima, Dima . . . where is my watering can?
DIMA: The monthly payment from Father came this
           morning.
NATHALIE: Put it in the drawer of my desk, Cactophil.
           Where is my blue watering can?
DIMA: I'll show you, Mother. Isabelle, if the pond isn't
           cleared, the trout will die!

Dima guides his mother towards the kitchen garden.

AUGUSTIN: One day I am going to make him swallow his
           bloody cactus.

Vava approaches from the house. Slow, dressed in black. He
bends down to tie up the laces of one of his heavy walking boots.
He points at Augustin.

VAVA: There he is! The Count Rostovski who is going
           to find himself in prison for debt! All
           decadence is due to the false distinction made
           between intellectual and manual labour.
           Leisure should be repose after work, when the
           body is grateful . . . Clean out the fish pond!

Meekly, the two grown-up children obey. They throw meal on the
water of the pond, and scoop out the fish in large nets with long

145

handles. The fish, as they are pulled out of the water, try to leap back.

ISABELLE:	Let's leave. Let's get the hell out of here.
AUGUSTIN:	The world outside is more ignoble than you think.
ISABELLE:	Ignoble! What a word. We'll go together, Tiny, we'll learn together.
AUGUSTIN:	Back to St Petersburg?
ISABELLE:	To the pyramids, to the Sphinx.
AUGUSTIN:	Dreams!

Isabelle empties a netful of fish into another section of the pond.

ISABELLE:	This family is doomed – I'm telling you, Tiny, for the last time. It has no roots – it is like one of the Cactophil's cactuses.
AUGUSTIN:	The plural is cacti!

NATHALIE'S BEDROOM – VILLA NUOVA, NIGHT

Single bed with brass fittings, lace pillowcases, gilt bedspread – but none of it is very clean. A writing bureau with scattered papers. In a corner several icons on the wall and a lighted candle before them. Nathalie, in her dressing-gown, is seated before a table with playing cards arranged as for a game of solitaire. Also on the table, an oil lamp, turned down low. Vava is seated opposite her.

NATHALIE:	The month's money from our Benefactor has come, my dear.
VAVA:	Benefactor!
NATHALIE:	We'd be lost without General Rostovski's roubles.
VAVA:	The Benefactor, as you always call him, pursues us even here.
NATHALIE:	By sending us money?
VAVA:	Through the pitiless laws of heredity – as demonstrated in his and your children!
NATHALIE:	Sometimes, Vava, you seem to forget how once you were my lover, a very passionate lover.

146

Vava gets up abruptly and goes to the window, perhaps to hide his feelings. Nathalie continues with her game of solitaire.

> NATHALIE: For days now the cards haven't been coming out.

Nathalie sighs, looks at the candle burning by the icons, and speaks as if to herself.

> NATHALIE: Christ aids those who suffer . . .
> VAVA: In the whole history of the human spirit there has been no greater abomination than Christ.
> NATHALIE: It's not kind of you to make such remarks, Alexander. Without Christ, men would have remained animals.
> VAVA: Men HAVE remained animals.
> NATHALIE: The money's in the drawer. Take it.

Vava pockets the envelope, leaves. Nathalie shuffles the cards.

DINING HALL, VILLA NUOVA

The room in the house where guests meet and talk. Lit by gaslight from the ceiling. The only furniture is a long wooden table with benches. On the wall behind, a large unfinished mural-painting depicting from left to right the Ascent of Man, according to Darwinian theory. The early phases (reptiles, mammals) are complete. Somewhere near the middle, the painting has stopped with Australopithecus Man. The other walls of the room are whitewashed, with signs of damp.

Vava sits at the head of the table, surrounded by Russian emigrés. Among them, Anya with a pince-nez and a stylish mauve dress, a Young Man with a student cap, and Vera, a young medical student. She is wearing a chaste brown frock with a little lace around the collar and sleeves.

> ANYA: He was arrested in St Petersburg, in a photography shop off the Haymarket.

YOUNG MAN: Executed the week after Easter . . . twenty-seven
years old. Obstinate about two things: Karl
Marx and his beard.

ANYA: How many times did I try to tell him? With a
beard like that, I told him, you're asking to be
picked up . . .

Enter Isabelle, dressed in her Russian peasant outfit, with a tray
of tea cups.

VAVA: What a waste of a life! At the time of Christ,
people were waiting for the end of the world; in
the Middle Ages they believed in the
imminence of the Last Judgement. For you, it's
the Revolution that will destroy all evil.

YOUNG MAN: He was twenty-seven!

Vava notices Isabelle. His face lights up.

VAVA: Isabelle, my child!

ANYA: Your daughter!

VAVA: My only child, whom I call Diogenes in the
conviction that she will follow the example of
that incorruptible philosopher.

ANYA: Why on earth does she dress like a man?

VAVA: I insist upon it. Dressed as a woman she'd be
treated as a member of the weaker sex. I want
her to be somebody who never hesitates to do
what needs to be done. I want nothing to make
her weak.

YOUNG MAN: Since the assassination in March, they've
recruited thousands of informers. They are
everywhere. Not only your concierge, but your
shoemaker, your coal merchant . . .

VERA: How do they make informers? How do they
break their pride so easily?

Vera's words are lost in her coughing. Still coughing, she moves
away from the table; Isabelle guides her to a bench by the kitchen
door. Anya gets up to inspect the painting on the wall.

ANYA: Who is the painter?
ISABELLE: Papa is the painter but he can't finish it: it's a question of faith.

Isabelle arranges a coat around Vera's shoulders.

YOUNG MAN: Things are changing in Russia; perhaps you don't realize it here.

Vera leans her head back against Isabelle's arm, closes her eyes.

ISABELLE: We'll go to the mountains together . . .
YOUNG MAN: The days of useless self-sacrifice are over.
VERA: When I've passed the exam, we'll go to the mountains . . . not before.

ISABELLE'S ROOM, VILLA NUOVA

The room is austere and untidy. A narrow bed without a pillow. A large table covered with notebooks and pages of writing. On one of the walls, a painting of a minaret. Beside the painting, a mirror. Isabelle, in her nightdress, gets up from the table and takes a white cloth out of a drawer and, in front of the mirror, puts it on like a turban.

Through the window, the cry of an owl. Furtively, the door opens. In the mirror, Isabelle sees Augustin, a little drunk. He is wearing a suit, white shirt, black silk scarf. He smiles.

ISABELLE: It's almost morning.
AUGUSTIN: Here's all I won. My luck's left me. Do you want them?

He comes up behind her and places a bank note on each of her shoulders. She shrugs her shoulders so the notes fall.

ISABELLE: Do you like my turban?

He adjusts her headdress and glances idly at some of the written papers on the table. He holds up a page, reading out loud.

149

AUGUSTIN: 'My dear Eugène, I feel in my heart that I have
             loved you for so long, since long, long before
             God created the world.'

Isabelle, furious, pushes him away from the table and tries to
seize the letter.

ISABELLE: You dare to read my letters! Who do you think
             you are!

Augustin jumps on to and off the bed, still holding the letter.

AUGUSTIN: 'Since long, long before God created the world
             . . . I feel in my heart that I have loved you . . .'

Isabelle finally grabs the letter and slaps his face. He takes her in
his arms.

ISABELLE: You remember, I told you about his
             advertisement in the French newspaper.
             'French officer in the Sahara, bored to death,
             would like to correspond with a young lady in
             Europe.' He's been writing to me for a year.
             I've never seen him. He's stationed in El Oued.
AUGUSTIN: And he's called Eugène?
ISABELLE: Eugène Letard . . . Tiny, you are jealous, aren't
             you? Yet there's no reason; you are still the love
             of my life.

She kisses him on the mouth.

COUNTRYSIDE NEAR VILLA NUOVA – SUMMER MORNING

Isabelle, dressed in her Russian peasant clothes, and her father
are on horseback. Both are holding open books in their hands.
The horses walk side by side; she is listening to her father.

VAVA: The man who first discovered tuberculosis to
             be infectious was Avicenna in the tenth century.
             What was his Islamic name?

150

ISABELLE: Ibn Sina.

As she answers, she triumphantly spurs her horse and gallops off, then she reins in and waits for her father, trotting to join her.

VAVA: Your essay was better than last week. But if you are going to talk about treachery, you must insist on how treachery is Shakespeare's favourite theme. Love between two, treachery between many! This was his vision. In every play he shows us treachery. We'll read Act I, Scene 4, of *King Lear* together.

They approach the house. Isabelle dismounts and holds her father's horse for him.

VAVA: I'll get our Shakespeare.

On his way to the house, he stops to tie up a lace. Isabelle watches him tenderly.

VAVA'S STUDY, VILLA NUOVA

Bookcases to the ceiling. A single sofa-bed. A large sepia portrait of Tolstoi. Many plants in pots. Augustin is standing on tiptoe by the bed, looking for something on the top bookshelf. Suddenly the door opens. It is Vava. Augustin jumps off the bed and looks guilty.

VAVA: You bastard! You'd steal from your own mother to pay for your filthy gambling.
AUGUSTIN: I needed . . .
VAVA: Liar!

Vava seizes Augustin by the collar and shakes him.

VAVA: It's not money! No. No! It's names, my God. Names!

Vava hits Augustin.

VAVA: You're looking for names. You're spying for the
         Czar!

Vava throws Augustin to the floor. Augustin scarcely resists. The
older man sits on top of him, seizes his shoulders, bangs his head
against the floor.

VAVA: I want the truth! Do you hear me? The truth.
AUGUSTIN: Isabelle! Isabelle! He's gone mad.
VAVA: Judas!

Nathalie enters in her dressing-gown, hair loose.

NATHALIE: Stop it, Alexander, I beg you to stop it. Stop!
VAVA: Do you know what the Benefactor's son was
          doing? Tell your mother! Tell it!
NATHALIE: My God. My God . . . you will kill him.

Nathalie collapses and crawls towards the sofa.

AUGUSTIN: Isabelle! Isabelle!

Isabelle enters, running, and places her hand on Vava's head; he
grasps her hand and becomes calm.

ISABELLE: Father, let Tiny get up.

Augustin rises to his feet, wipes the blood from his face. Dima is
standing in the doorway.

DIMA: He'd steal money, Father, but not names, not
          yet . . .

Augustin leaves the room without a word. Nathalie sniffs some
smelling salts. Vava leans back in a chair, hands hanging by his
sides.

VAVA: We are primitives, Diogenes, primitives because
          we are among the first . . . We are clumsy,
          violent . . . too passionate. Others will come
          after us who will be better prepared to realize
          our ideal. History does not advance like a

152

locomotive, but like a glacier. For all the heat
of our passion, my beloved, history is cold. So
cold . . .

Nathalie struggles to her feet. Isabelle looks anxiously at Vava
slumped in his chair.

> DIMA: Go with Mother, I'll stay with him.

Isabelle leads her mother out of the room.

HALLWAY STAIRCASE

On the staircase, Nathalie moans like a child.

> NATHALIE: Take me away from here. I can't stand it any
> more . . . he wanted to kill my son. Take me
> away, I'll never leave them, but just for a while .
> . . Take me away for a little while . . .

SHIP'S CABIN – AT SEA – NIGHT

The cabin is comfortable with two bunks. Hanging objects swing
as the ship rolls. Nathalie is lying fully dressed on her bunk.
Isabelle, in a white dress, is writing in a notebook. When Nathalie
speaks, Isabelle does not immediately look up; she wants to be
left in peace.

> NATHALIE: The first time I saw your father, the coach had
> stopped in front of the house with white
> columns and his overcoat was covered with
> dust. He came to tutor Dima and Augustin. The
> general was away on manoeuvres . . . I fell in
> love with him at first sight. To love like I loved
> him is terrible . . . one should never love like
> that, one should never go away, one should
> never leave . . . one should stay.

Isabelle puts aside her notebook and speaks as if to a child.

ISABELLE:	We'll go back to the Villa Nuova, Mother. We're only away for the winter.
NATHALIE:	When people start crossing seas, they never come back at the right moment –
ISABELLE:	Don't go on, *Maman*. You need a rest and a change.
NATHALIE:	The hot climate in Algeria may not be good for my heart.
ISABELLE:	The houses are cool. You don't realize how lucky we are to have been lent this house – there's a verandah overlooking the sea, a well in the garden, palm trees . . . This little house in Bone was meant for us. Mektoub!
NATHALIE:	What?
ISABELLE:	Do you know what that means, Mother? It means: It has been written.
NATHALIE:	How. . . ?
ISABELLE:	When God created the pen he commanded it to write. Write down the destiny of all things, he said, all things to the end of the world.

Nathalie is asleep.

SHIP'S DECK

Isabelle descends a metal staircase to the crowded fourth-class deck, where the passengers, almost all of them North African, have improvised shelters against the wind and are sitting or sprawling on the deck. Many of the women are veiled. Some of the men are smoking narghiles. An unveiled woman, over fifty, wearing earrings and bracelets, holds out her hand as Isabelle passes. It could be the gesture of a beggar; Isabelle takes it as such and modestly looks for a coin. As she does so, she says in Arabic: 'Allahou Akbar!' The woman clasps Isabelle's hand to invite her to sit down beside her. Her name is Lella Hadra.

LELLA HADRA:	Stay. What I have to tell you is for your two ears, not for the brass ear of money. In the poor mountains there lived a Bedouin shepherd girl called Smina. One day a French officer, a

Roumi, asked her for water to give to his horse
to drink. This Roumi officer fell in love with
Smina – her eyes were like damsons. She said
she could love him only if he became a Muslim
. . . He took the oath and she named him
Mabrouk. Smina's love for her Mabrouk was
blind, yet she knew he would leave her. 'Next
week I must go,' he said. 'I will come back
soon.' And she replied: 'You want me no more,
Mabrouk, you want to keep neither me nor
your own word.'

Isabelle sips a glass of mint tea that has been offered to her.

LELLA HADRA: He left to become a major in his army, and he
               married a Roumia as all Roumis do.
ISABELLE: And Smina?
LELLA HADRA: She remained faithful to her love, she danced
               in cabarets, she became a camp-follower. She
               waits for her master to come back . . . When he
               comes back she will tell him he is a dog, a son
               of a bitch, who can love neither word nor
               woman, and as she says this her eyes – all
               wrinkled now – will . . .
ISABELLE: Will?
LELLA HADRA: . . . will look upon the life they never lived.

BACKSTREET – BONE, ALGERIA – AFTERNOON

The Arab quarter. Barefoot children, women in black robes,
mostly veiled. Merchants. Beggars. Isabelle is dressed in a white
burnous and a turban. Stops before a small moorish cafe, peers
through the bead curtains. In an alcove a group of Foreign
Legionnaires sprawling on carpets on the floor. An Arab flute
player. A boy serving coffee. Several empty tables. Seated at one is
Lella Hadra. Isabelle enters. The habitués glance at her only for a
moment – they take her to be an unknown Arab boy.

ISABELLE: Why did you tell me the story of Smina?

155

Lella recognizes her voice.

> LELLA: Because a word said is a word given.

Lella is wearing more bracelets than on the boat, and a silver-threaded headscarf. She uses this cafe as her office. She foresees the future, undoes spells, and sells *dawamesk* (a pastry containing cannabis). On the table in front of her are envelopes and small packets of *dawamesk*.

> ISABELLE: Is there nothing more written for me?
> LELLA: Everything is written, but not everything can be read at once. You must return.

Isabelle takes out a cigarette, has no light. Lella nods in the direction of the Legionnaires. A Legionnaire strikes a match.

> LEGIONNAIRE: I knew a man from Bou Saada who tried to light a cigarette with a pistol shot. He blinded himself.
> ISABELLE: The disadvantages of being alone!
> LEGIONNAIRE: You've seen the old woman's pastries? Spread with happiness those ones are . . .

Isabelle takes two *dawamesk*. Lella refuses any money. Isabelle lies on the carpet near the Legionnaires.

> ISABELLE: I want to go to El Oued.
> LEGIONNAIRE: What's your name?
> ISABELLE: Mahmoud. I come from Tunis.
> LEGIONNAIRE: Bring us a pastry and we'll tell you about El Oued.

The Arab flute continues. Isabelle slips into the arms of a Legionnaire, pulls his face towards her and kisses him on the mouth. He is surprised to discover that she is a woman.

Lella observes the scene. With a small kerchief she wipes her cheek.

TERRACE OF SMALL HOUSE – BONE – EARLY MORNING

Winter sunlight. Nathalie is scattering bread crumbs for birds along the balustrade. Then, wrapped in a blanket, she lies in a deck-chair with her feet up. On the table beside her is a glass of tea. She closes her eyes. Her face is drawn.

Isabelle appears in the doorway that opens onto the terrace from the living room. She is wearing her male Arab clothes She has removed her sandals; her feet are dirty.

NATHALIE: You've been out all night, my child.
ISABELLE: How are you, Mother?
NATHALIE: I couldn't sleep.

Isabelle sits on the floor beside the deck-chair and rests her head on her mother's lap.

NATHALIE: I'm worried about you, you're not looking well. And why do you dress like this every night?
ISABELLE: Do you know what I call you when I can't see you, Mother? I call you my White Angel.
NATHALIE: Your breath smells of drink . . . and you are my youngest.
ISABELLE: I'm older than any of you think.

Isabelle moves away from the deck-chair and lies down on the terrace, looking up at the sky.

NATHALIE: Every night you disappear.
ISABELLE: We're going to leave this wretched, small-minded Bone, Mother. We're going to go to El Oued!
NATHALIE: It's not as if this were our own country.
ISABELLE: We'll learn how to live on this earth . . .
NATHALIE: The General was kind to me, you know that? He was tolerant, he was so tolerant . . .
ISABELLE: Sleep, Mother, sleep.

Both fall asleep. One on the ground; one in the deck-chair. Pigeons alight on the balustrade and eat the bread crumbs.

SAME TERRACE AT MIDDAY

An Algerian woman servant opens the French windows onto the terrace. Isabelle and Nathalie are still asleep. Putting down her tray, the servant goes over to the deck-chair and says: 'Madame.' She touches the shoulder of the old lady. Silence. Then the servant screams. Nothing stirs. Not even Isabelle. Nathalie is dead.

DINING HALL, VILLA NUOVA – AFTERNOON

Outside, the trees are heavy with snow. Vava, visibly older, with unkempt beard, a blanket over his shoulders, is working on his mural painting, adding flowers along the lower edge. Dima crosses the room, wearing gloves and overcoat. He is carrying a large cactus in a pot, which obliges him to walk with his chin held high, as if blind to everything around him. Isabelle, wearing Vera's student frock, is curled up in a corner on the floor. Her sobs become louder. Vava puts down his brushes.

> ISABELLE: Without her I don't want to live!

Vava opens the drawer of the table and takes out a revolver, a nickel-plated six-chamber Colt with an inset ivory handpiece. He loads it.

> VAVA: Stand up!

Isabelle gets to her feet and stands at the far end of the long table. Vava walks slowly towards her, holding out the revolver, muzzle towards himself.

> VAVA: So you don't want to live? One should always be clear about what one wants! To choose is to be free.

He places the revolver on the table in front of Isabelle. She lowers her hands from her face and stares at the weapon. Nobody moves or speaks. Isabelle begins to laugh. Dima approaches the table, picks up the revolver, and blows lightly across its mouth as if to get rid of a cobweb. When he replaces it on the table, Isabelle picks it up.

Then she notices Vava. The old man's eyes are filled with tears.

ISABELLE: It will be all right, Father. All right. I promise.

GARDEN OF VILLA NUOVA – MORNING

Blue sky above the snow. A suitcase stands by the fish pond. Isabelle, wearing an overcoat, is testing the strength of the ice with her foot. Tentatively she tries her weight. Sure of herself, she runs and slides, as she did as a child.

Dima emerges from behind a shack and watches. Suddenly her feet slip and she falls. She tries to get up, and cannot.

DIMA: She was my mother just as she was yours . . . She loved you but she trusted me. One by one you all go. If you hadn't taken her to Bone, she would still be alive . . .

Isabelle turns, still sitting on the ice, to face him. With her hand she shields her eyes from the sun.

ISABELLE: It's too late, Cactophil . . . all we can do now is mourn.

Dima shouts, partly to bridge the distance, partly in rage.

DIMA: You all leave and you don't even know where and why you're going . . . you're going to your ruin. Look at Brother Augustin, eking out a living in Marseille and married to a shopkeeper's daughter who is nibbling him away, crumb by crumb . . . And you – why don't you fill your notebooks with your poetic dreams here, in the only house that will ever be yours, instead of trying to live them out in the murderous world? Vava can still make it from his bed to his books. He couldn't survive a day by himself. Every night he takes morphine, more and more. I should know because I get it for him. Sometimes he's doubled up with pain.

159

Isabelle approaches her brother over the ice and kisses him on both cheeks.

> DIMA: Without you, we'll both die . . . there'll be no more sense in this house.

Isabelle picks up her suitcase.

> ISABELLE: Forgive me, Dima, forgive me. I can't help it. I have to go.
>
> DIMA: Do you know what you're looking for? You're looking for a garden, aren't you? and there's one right here!

Original line drawing by Isabelle Eberhardt

Act 2

MARSEILLE DOCKS – LATE AFTERNOON, SEPTEMBER 1898

Cranes. Derricks. Train wagons. Horses. From the hold of the nearest ship a dozen longshoremen carry sacks of beans down a gangplank and across the cobbles to a train wagon. The file is made up of Europeans and North Africans. All wear similar European work-clothes, the North Africans distinguished by their turbans. Among them, dressed as a man, is Isabelle.

As she descends the gangplank with a heavy sack across her shoulders, the Arab in front of her, on reaching the cobbled quayside, lowers his sack to the ground, takes two steps to the side and prostrates himself to recite a prayer. Isabelle hesitates. Should she warn the man? The Italian docker behind slaps her on the shoulder and they continue with their sacks towards the wagon. The Foreman, holding a wad of invoices, hurries towards the Arab.

> FOREMAN: What the hell do you think you're doing? Who gave you permission? You're in France now. In France we work, we don't pray while working. When we pray, we go to church, and when we work, you son of a whore, we work!

The man gets to his feet. The others who have unloaded their sacks are returning to the ship. Isabelle turns around and slaps her arm in an obscene gesture at the foreman.

TENEMENT KITCHEN – MARSEILLE – NIGHT

The room is ill-lit. Laundry hangs over the stove. Augustin is sitting at the kitchen table. Spread out on the table are conches and other seashells. He is gluing these together to make ornaments to sell to sailors and tourists.

Jenny, his wife, is in a dressing-gown. She has a buxom figure, a small mouth and shrill voice. She is feeling the laundry with her hand.

> JENNY: With this goddamned cold, it'll never dry! I need it to change Baby in the morning. And you, what do you care? You and your seashells.

	Why don't you try selling insurance like my friend suggested?
AUGUSTIN:	I'd rather go back and work on the docks than do that.
JENNY:	Too proud?
AUGUSTIN:	I've never seen such a small shell as this one.
JENNY:	Ah! You aristocrat! And now there are two of you. Little sister turns up, all smiles and kisses, and without a penny to her name. Eats every evening, scribbles every night, smokes kif and never lifts a finger to help in the kitchen. You are both the same: you think the world owes you a living!
AUGUSTIN:	I sell my shells.
JENNY:	One doesn't even know if she's a man or woman. Fish or fowl.
AUGUSTIN:	The eye of the hermit crab is the most primitive in the whole history of evolution. Only forty cones.
JENNY:	Cones!

Isabelle, in her work clothes, comes in. She unwinds her scarf. Her face and hands are very dirty. Taking some money out of her pocket, she is about to place it on the table.

JENNY:	Don't touch that cloth with your filthy hands!

Isabelle, with the gesture of a conjuror, lets the banknotes and coins fall one by one onto the tablecloth.

ISABELLE:	What's wrong with the mistress of the house today? It's clean money!

Jenny leaves to attend to the baby in the next room. She slams the door behind her.

AUGUSTIN:	There's a letter for you.
ISABELLE:	Where from?
AUGUSTIN:	Algeria.

Isabelle unbuttons her shirt to wash at the sink. Augustin turns the envelope over.

AUGUSTIN: It's from your postal lover – the Lieutenant!

Isabelle is washing under the tap. Augustin looks intently at her naked torso and picks up a seashell.

AUGUSTIN: Shellfish, unlike us, are never homeless. You have beautiful breasts.

Isabelle turns around from the sink and sadly shakes her head.

ISABELLE: Do you think you've made a mistake, Tiny, about your home?
AUGUSTIN: Life is a mistake, little sister.

Jenny comes into the kitchen to get a diaper. She eyes the two of them with suspicion and leaves.

ISABELLE: Read me Eugène's letter.

Augustin opens the envelope with a paperknife.

AUGUSTIN: It's short. He calls you his Gazelle. He's left El Oued and he invites you to Bone, where he's now stationed.

Isabelle laughs. Augustin fingers another shell.

'BAR IDEAL' – MARSEILLE – NIGHT

Large wooden tables, and around one of them, already drinking, a group of Longshoremen and Fishermen. They make signs for Isabelle to join them. They know her as Mahmoud from Tunis.

FISHERMAN: You can try a different jetty, he's always there, King Rat, and he doesn't live on board, he lives on land. One day I say to myself, I've had enough of this. So, I throw King Rat nothing. I ignore him. He waits one minute, he gives a sign to his gang of rats, and they swarm over the deck and over the whole catch. Every fish mauled. I had to sell the catch at half-price.

LONGSHOREMAN:	In the docks, King Rat walks on two legs. You stop to have a piss and there he is! Sitting up and watching you, and you haven't had time to button up your trousers.
LONGSHOREMAN:	The Berry docks Monday next – clean wood, not coal shit like the last lot. If we grease the Rat, there's work guaranteed for four days. What do you say, Mahmoud, are you coming in with us?

By way of reply, Isabelle hands some money to the bartender. A bottle of absinthe arrives with a saucer of sugar. The dockers slap her on her back.

LONGSHOREMAN:	And the Berry Docks next Monday? We'll count you in?
ISABELLE:	I'm leaving the City of Rats.
LONGSHOREMAN:	Who wouldn't?
ISABELLE:	Monday I'll be in Algeria.

QUAYSIDE – BONE, ALGERIA – MORNING

A ship has docked. The quayside is crowded with people: porters, customs officials, and those waiting to meet friends or relatives. A band is playing. The passengers descend by two gangways: one for cabin passengers, and the other for the Fourth Class who slept on deck.

The crowd on the dockside is likewise divided: the Europeans are gathered around a tall flagpole with a tricolour; the North Africans form a group apart, near the stern of the ship. The sky is full of gulls.

Nearer the water's edge than most of the Europeans stands a junior officer. This is Captain Eugène Letord. He eyes inquiringly each passenger who comes down the Cabin Class gangway.

By the flagpole stands a senior French officer. This is Colonel Lyautey.

Isabelle, dressed as Mahmoud, has already come down the Fourth

Class gangway. She has a bundle slung over her shoulder, walks casually between the boat and the Europeans, cigarette in mouth. Whenever she spots a young officer, she briefly studies his face. Certain Europeans, particularly the women, glance at her with suspicion. Their question can be read on their faces: What does this street-Arab think he is doing staring at us?

Lyautey is following the 'street-Arab' with rapt interest. The well-dressed elderly lady, for whom he was waiting, comes within arms' length before he turns to recognize and greet her.

Meanwhile, Isabelle has identified Eugène and is standing a few yards away, watching him as he studies each passenger coming down the gangway.

> ISABELLE: 'Young officer, stationed in the Sahara, bored to death, seeks correspondent.'

Eugène spins around flabbergasted.

> ISABELLE: Eugène!
> EUGÈNE: Never! It can't be.
> ISABELLE: You're even thinner than your handwriting!
> EUGÈNE: Isabelle?

Clumsily, shyly, he takes her hand and kisses it. Nothing about this encounter between a young captain and a street-Arab has escaped Lyautey.

> EUGÈNE: We must get your luggage.

Isabelle makes a sign to show that she has nothing but the bundle she carries over her shoulder.

> EUGÈNE: Not even a dress?
> ISABELLE: I left everything behind, dresses included. Your Isabelle has gone. You are looking at Mahmoud Essadi, a student of the Koran from Tunis.

She pauses, as if to give them both time to think of who she is under her clothes and without a name.

ISABELLE: . . . only son of a tailor.
EUGÈNE: And Isabelle Eberhardt?
ISABELLE: You have to invent her.

Eugène and Isabelle walk along the quayside, past workers, camels, mules. Their progress is awkward because Isabelle keeps stopping in her tracks to look at him. He is carrying her bundle.

EUGÈNE: There are so many things I want to ask you . . .

A child comes up to Eugène to beg. A porter, bent like a jack-knife and carrying an immense pile of leather hides on his back, his face parallel to the ground, passes between them.

AN ARCADE WITH LUXURY SHOPS

On the faces of those who pass the French officer and his street-Arab companion can be read surprise, disapproval, consternation, outrage.

EUGÈNE: I've never heard your voice in my life, but when you pronounced my name I knew it was you immediately. It was the voice of your letters, your letters which I've read like music for so many years.

Isabelle stops before a saddler's shop.

ISABELLE: Do you ride with long or short stirrups?
EUGÈNE: Not too short.
ISABELLE: There's a Persian saying: 'As you wear your stirrups out, you ought to understand the world better.' I like that, don't you?
EUGÈNE: May I take Mahmoud Essadi shopping?
ISABELLE: What shall we do about his hair?
EUGÈNE: We'll find him a hat.
ISABELLE: And when he takes his hat off?
EUGÈNE: He'll be wearing a wig!

HOTEL BEDROOM – BONE – EARLY EVENING

On the walls hang several large oil paintings depicting Oriental
scenes: the bazaar, a harem, a Biblical event.

Everywhere – on the floor, on the bed, on the table, in the
armchairs – are packets, cardboard boxes, tissue paper, feminine
underclothes, hats, shoes, etc. The door to the bathroom is ajar.
Eugène, lolling in a chair, is sipping a pastis and smoking a
cigarette. Isabelle is in the bathroom.

> EUGÈNE: Sometimes I used to think I was going to die of
> boredom here.
>
> ISABELLE: What did you say?
>
> EUGÈNE: I said: One dies of boredom in these garrison
> towns: Bone, Ain Sefra, Batna.
>
> ISABELLE: Boredom? Why?

The sound of running water stops.

> EUGÈNE: There's nothing to do. Sometimes for days,
> weeks on end. Not even with 'manoeuvres'. So
> I smoke kif. It stops you thinking . . . it cradles
> you . . . a return to childhood. But with you
> here, all that will change.
>
> ISABELLE: Kif by itself is nothing. It gets interesting when
> you mix it with absinthe.
>
> EUGÈNE: I want you to meet a few people here: Jacques
> Lacoste – he runs a literary magazine. Simon
> Lazare, a poet. I've read them passages from
> your letters, and they admire your writing.
>
> ISABELLE: Writing! A writer is someone who betrays his
> best friend, then writes an immortal page on
> the nature of treachery.
>
> EUGÈNE: And above all, I want you to meet Louis Hubert
> Lyautey.

Isabelle, still in the bathroom, is ruffling the wig, prior to putting
it on.

> ISABELLE: Who is Lyautey?
>
> EUGÈNE: Our great and famous colonel . . . a soldier of

genius such as you get once in a century. A man of reason and a romantic. A believer, and what he believes in is action.

Isabelle appears in the doorway, impeccably dressed, coiffed, poised. White dress bordered with lace, white stockings, black shoes. For a moment she stands framed in the doorway, as if posing for Eugene.

ISABELLE: What is he doing here, your romantic who believes in action?

EUGÈNE: He's on a visit from Indo-China. He's going to build an empire – of a new kind.

ISABELLE: A colonel?

EUGÈNE: I'm certain you'll have a lot to say to each other.

She sweeps some underwear off one of the armchairs and sits on it.

ISABELLE: Yet another empire . . . Soon we'll all be dead! Did you know that? Dead! My poor Eugène. Am I easier to read than to be with?

A GARDEN – BONE – EARLY EVENING

Thirty or so guests assembled for a garden party. Algerian servants. Buffet tables. Food and drink. Exotic plants. A raised terrace at one end of the garden, on which there is a grand piano. At the other end, an animal cage housing birds and zebras.

Eugene guides Isabelle between the standing guests, his hand under her elbow, introducing her. They approach Colonel Lyautey.

LYAUTEY: And so you are the charming Isabelle. Eugene has read me some of your wonderful letters, Isabelle, if I may take the liberty of using your Christian name?

ISABELLE: Already in my life, sir, I have had many names.

LYAUTEY:	There are honourable reasons for changing one's name – even one's identity – and there are dishonourable ones. I am certain, my dear Isabelle, that your reasons have always been of the former kind.
ISABELLE:	In the end every name is effaced by time and the sand, isn't it?
LYAUTEY:	We all want to leave something behind, don't you think?
ISABELLE:	So little. Do you dream, sir?
LYAUTEY:	Yes, I have a dream, a dream to establish for as long as possible a little order, a little peace.
ISABELLE:	Whose peace? The order of what?
EUGÈNE:	The Marquise de Chamalliere is here, my Colonel.
LYAUTEY:	Our story, Miss Eberhardt – for we both provoke stories, don't we – our story is not yet over.

Eugène presents Isabelle to other guests.

SPORTSMAN:	Eugène mentioned that you are a keen horsewoman, Miss Eberhardt. Fast horses are the only good thing they have in this God-forsaken country.

An Officer approaches Eugène.

OFFICER:	The Colonel would like to see you for a moment.

Eugène turns to Isabelle.

EUGÈNE:	Duty calls.

A Young Woman approaches Isabelle.

YOUNG WOMAN:	Eugène said you can speak at least five languages.
ISABELLE:	My father was a very good teacher.
YOUNG WOMAN:	Do you like rugs?
ISABELLE:	Rugs?

173

YOUNG WOMAN: Prayer mats. I've become absolutely fascinated
by them, and we go to the bazaar to buy them.
We'd love you to come with us, and with you
speaking their lingo, we'll get a bargain.

Someone starts to play a piano. The zebras in the cage raise their
heads.

ELDERLY WOMAN: I hear you are a writer. What kind of books do
you write? Romances? Adventure stories?
ISABELLE: Epitaphs, Madame.

Lamps in the garden are lit. Eugène is seated at the piano. He
looks anxiously to see where Isabelle is.

Isabelle is sitting alone in a chair, at the end of the garden.
Nearby, a group of officers, a little tipsy; among them, Captain
Frioux. They are talking about Isabelle.

AN OFFICER: They say she is of Russian origin, the daughter
of a general in the Czar's army.
FRIOUX: I can just see Eugène as the son-in-law of a
Russian general!

Captain Frioux approaches Isabelle with a gallant gesture.

FRIOUX: May I offer you a glass of champagne?

The Officers perform for her the ritual of 'beheading' one, two,
three bottles. With a single blow they cut off the neck of each
bottle with a sabre. Froth spurts up and over the table. Captain
Frioux offers Isabelle a glass.

VOICE: Ladies and Gentlemen! I have the honour of
announcing that Colonel Lyautey has
consented to sing for us.

Isabelle sips her champagne and speaks to Captain Frioux.

ISABELLE: Are you stationed in Bone, Captain?
FRIOUX: Just visiting. Tomorrow I have to go south again
and hunt down the latest trouble-makers.

174

ISABELLE: You are in the cavalry?
FRIOUX: Intelligence, Madame, the Arab Bureau. We
              find out who's pulling the strings. In this case
              it's the Qadrya.
ISABELLE: The Qadrya?
FRIOUX: Fanatics. You have heard of Emir Abdelkader?
              He thought he could change the world – until
              we sent him to Toulon. He was a Qadrya.

The first notes of the piano, played by Eugène. Frioux rejoins the
other officers to watch Lyautey.

FRIOUX: In Indo-China he behaves like Julius Caesar,
              and here he thinks he's Rigoletto.

Lyautey stands very upright beside the piano. His eyes are shut –
as though in prayer. He sings a Schubert lieder. The guests
compose their faces to listen solemnly.

Isabelle, glass in hand, listens to the quavering voice. Everyone's
back is turned to her. She studies Lyautey, lost in thought. Then
she sighs and, with a single gesture, removes her wig, rubs her
hair and lights a cigarette. An Algerian waiter is watching her.

ISABELLE: Is it always like this when they give a party?

The waiter shrugs his shoulders.

ISABELLE: From the back of the garden, can you get out
              into the street?

The waiter explains with gestures. Isabelle thanks him in Arabic.

Lyautey is enchanted by the music and by the attention of his
audience. Eugène, while accompanying him on the piano, sees
Isabelle leave through the back door. Lyautey reaches the last
tremulously held note. Clapping. Cries of 'Encore!'

HOTEL BEDROOM – BONE – MORNING

Isabelle is sorting out her bundle of possessions. Wearing her Arab man's trousers and a cotton shirt, she is standing barefoot at a small round table. In front of her, spread on this table, are her notebooks, a bundle of letters, a djellaba and, wrapped in a beaded cloth, her revolver. She takes some of these things and arranges them in the drawer of the dressing table. She picks up a burnous and begins to move across the room.

She approaches one of the oil paintings: a portrayal of a holy man – more from the Bible than the Koran. Isabelle peers at it and then wraps the burnous around her head, in a parody of the portrait. Then she takes the burnous and drapes it over the painting.

FRENCH ARMY HEADQUARTERS – BONE – DAWN

Eugène is running up a wide staircase. An old woman is washing the stairs.

Eugène pulls off his gloves and knocks lightly on a massive door with brass fittings. Enters. A large room with bookcases. The blinds are down so that only a little light filters in. Lyautey is seated at a table with breakfast, fruit, a vase of flowers, on a white tablecloth. He is wearing an embroidered dressing-gown over elegant pyjamas. On the table there is one unusual object: a gas burner with a flame at its tip. (Like a laboratory Bunsen burner but taller, more delicate and made of brass.)

Before Eugène arrived, Lyautey was reading a report. Now he takes off his glasses, beckons his friend to sit down, and lights a cigarette from the 'eternal flame' of the burner.

> LYAUTEY: I've always liked conversations over breakfast. So did your father. The milk's there. Our friend the other evening at the garden party, Miss Eberhardt, is a remarkable person. I offer you my congratulations.

Eugène shifts in his chair. Lyautey offers him a cigarette from a gold case, and indicates the 'eternal flame'.

LYAUTEY: In any case, it's the future I want to talk about.
              Now your father is dead, I feel I owe it to him
              to keep an eye on you.

Lyautey stands up and comes behind Eugène to place a hand on
his shoulder.

LYAUTEY: You are wasting your life here. You are living
              with clichés, military clichés, ethical clichés. In
              Indo-China, by contrast, we're making history.
              You would discover yourself with us out there,
              and you would live a life dedicated to . . . well,
              to something!

Lyautey strolls to the window and opens the blinds.

LYAUTEY: Another sunny day. Well, there's my offer,
              Eugène. Come to Indo-China. Come with us.

Eugène puts on his gloves. He is silent.

HOTEL BEDROOM – BONE – AFTERNOON

Eugène reclines dreamily in a steaming bath. Isabelle enters,
barefoot, tousled, wearing her brown student frock.

EUGÈNE: You're dressed already! I've never seen that
              frock.

Isabelle kneels down by the bath.

ISABELLE: I inherited it from a friend. Her name was
              Vera. She came from a small town in Russia and
              was studying medicine in Geneva.

Eugène stands up in the bath. Isabelle drapes the elaborate
Turkish towels around him. While doing so, she talks.

ISABELLE: Vera wanted to be a doctor. Her life was
              determined by this one thought, this one
              desire, to help people. She was near the end of

177

her studies . . . and she had tuberculosis. The exams were in October. By the end of September she couldn't even get out of bed. Every morning she asked me what date it was and made me promise that, on the day, I would take her to the exam. She died two days before she was due to take it. She was herself, until the last moment, truly herself.

They slowly walk into the bedroom. Eugène, wrapped in his towels, takes her into his arms.

EUGÈNE: Do you think I live with clichés?
ISABELLE: Why?
EUGÈNE: Here we're boxed in with clichés, everyday clichés, ethical clichés. Let us get away. I've thought out a plan for us. I want to leave the military. We could go to Quebec. It is the France of the coming century, and more than twice as large.
ISABELLE: No, Eugène, you don't understand.

She frees herself from his embrace. He sits down on the bed.

EUGÈNE: We'll discover a new world together, build our home, bring up our children.

Isabelle picks up his boots, tunic and kepi from the floor.

EUGÈNE: There'll be no more compromises.
ISABELLE: Quebec! What is it? A bit of France, a bit of Europe in yet another colony.
EUGÈNE: I thought this is what you wanted.

Isabelle abruptly throws all his uniform out of the door into the corridor.

ISABELLE: I know what I don't want. I know what I have to get away from!

Minutes pass in silence. There is a knock on the door, Isabelle opens it. A hotel Servant, with Eugène's tunic over his arm.

178

SERVANT: The boots will be cleaned. Do you want the tunic pressed, Madame?

Isabelle takes the tunic from the servant. Eugène is still on the bed. Isabelle holds the uniform in front of her.

ISABELLE: You all dream of the Great Civilisation! I can't see an order worth imposing. Whatever I'm looking for, I'll find it beyond your frontiers. If I find it anywhere, it will be in the wilderness, my wilderness, if I find it . . .

HOUSE OF A WEALTHY MERCHANT – BONE – AFTERNOON

A number of French officials have been invited to a reception by a wealthy merchant. Coffee and pastries are being served, and the host is making a speech to his guests in a room which gives onto a terrace. During the host's speech, Lyautey wanders onto the terrace. The terrace overlooks the outer courtyard of a small mosque, where there is an arcade and a fountain. Seated on a carpet in the courtyard, an old Arab is instructing three others sitting before him. One of the three is Isabelle, dressed as Mahmoud. Lyautey beckons to somebody in the room. Eugène comes out and Lyautey indicates to him the courtyard of the mosque.

LYAUTEY: Our student of the Koran has fascinating connections. No play-acting there.
EUGÈNE: She lives each moment as if it were her last.

The four Arabs below are reciting from the first chapter of the Koran.

VOICES: 'In the name of God who is Good and Merciful, praise to God . . . Lord of the Day of Judgement . . . it is You alone we adore, from You alone that we ask . . .'
LYAUTEY: Are you really sure she is a woman?
EUGÈNE: Yes, I'm sure.
LYAUTEY: And supposing, Eugène, you had come to know – by what shall we call them? The same

179

	disclosures? – that our student of the Koran was a man: would you be willing to tell me?
EUGÈNE:	Isabelle is a woman.

They both look down from the balustrade at the courtyard. They turn around when a Servant offers them coffee on a silver tray.

LYAUTEY:	It's a difficult choice for you, I know. It's between two kinds of freedom, isn't it? Ours, which comes with the flag and depends upon discipline and order. And hers, which is the thoughtless freedom of the nomad.
EUGÈNE:	Thoughtless? If only I knew half what she knows.
LYAUTEY:	Nobody, my dear boy, will ever be able to share her freedom with her.

OUTER COURTYARD OF MOSQUE

Eugène enters the courtyard, searching for Isabelle. Finally he spots her sitting at the mosque's fountain, washing her feet. Isabelle looks up.

ISABELLE:	What's the matter, Eugène?
EUGÈNE:	I have to leave. I've been posted to Indo-China. Tonkin.
ISABELLE:	It's Lyautey who is taking you?
EUGÈNE:	I didn't want to go, it all happened so quickly and now . . . I have to leave. I didn't have the courage to tell you face to face . . . your eyes make me feel like a coward.
ISABELLE:	A coward! You're out of your mind.
EUGÈNE:	I'll write to you.
ISABELLE:	We've written so many letters to each other, haven't we? So many . . . I'm leaving too. I'm leaving for the south. Perhaps I'm better in letters.

TERMINUS OF A RAILWAY LINE – DESERT – MORNING

In front of a train is a huddle of Arab passengers. Others are off-loading luggage. Several camels and their nomad herders sit on the ground.

Isabelle walks over to the men by the camels. The train backs out along the single line. Steam and smoke hang in the air, then begin to drift away. A vast desert landscape with dunes spreading towards the horizon.

There is no station; the train stopped at the track's end.

Isabelle sits down on a saddle. A Camel Driver addresses her.

CAMEL DRIVER:	Where have you come from?
ISABELLE:	From Tunis. And you?
CAMEL DRIVER:	El Oued.
ISABELLE:	I'm going to El Oued.
CAMEL DRIVER:	You go to Bordy Saada and from there to Bir Sthil and from there to El Mraiev and from there to El Magger and from El Magger to Touggourt, in Touggourt you get your pass stamped and you go to Temassine, after Temassine to Ferdyenn to Moiet-el-Caid and to Big Ourmes and the next day you arrive in El Oued.

SOUF DESERT – BEFORE SUNSET

Towards one horizon, dunes; towards another, sandy rocks. In a few places scrubs of drinn grass. A small nomad encampment, their wooden-framed tents already pitched for the night. A herd of sheep and goats. Some camels hobbled behind the tents. Near one of the tents an old man is seated, and near him, Isabelle, dressed as Mahmoud, is taking saddle bags off a mule. The Old Nomad is talking, as if almost to himself, but in fact to her.

OLD NOMAD:	The Qadrya, my little Tebbib, submit to God and to no one else. For twenty generations, twenty . . . their colour is green, the prophet's colour.

He shows her the green rosary he is wearing around his neck.
The old man is blind.

OLD NOMAD: If you want to learn, go to Sidi Lachmi, the
              marabout of Guemar. He is a sheik and a holy
              man. The tribes listen to his teachings as do the
              angels.

Three children approach, each holding a fistful of sand. In turn
they pour the sand into the blind man's hands. He feels and
weighs each fistful and pronounces.

OLD NOMAD: We're a day's journey west of the Chott of
              Djerid. There's drinn for the herd an hour to
              the south.

Far away, a rifle shot.

SOUF DESERT – BEFORE SUNSET

A small French convoy: one officer, four spahis on horseback and
two Arab prisoners, wrists bound, on foot. Shots ring out. Hidden
behind the ghourd of a dune, a Young Arab on horseback fires at
the convoy. Then he shouts and another Arab horseman appears
from behind another ghourd. Both men charge forward, firing
from the shoulder.

The Legionnaires leap from their horses and, kneeling, return
the fire. The officer draws his revolver. The prisoners shout to
their liberators. The Second Arab Horseman falls. The First
Horseman charges on and, in turn, is hit. His rifle drops, but he
is able to stay on his horse, which veers away towards the horizon.

NOMAD ENCAMPMENT – SOUF DESERT – EVENING

The Old Nomad, as before, is seated near a tent, but is now
alone. He recites to himself.

OLD NOMAD: A sandstorm of shots should never give us
              fright. Death is God's gift, his porter the bullets.

A horseman approaches.

HORSEMAN: May the Peace of God be with you.
OLD NOMAD: You are in the hands of God and then in mine.
              I will answer for you.

The Horseman slides from his horse to the ground. He is gravely
wounded and has no rifle. He is carried into a tent.

NOMAD'S TENT – NIGHT

The Horseman, laid out on a palliasse, is feverish and breathes
with difficulty. He is covered with a sheepskin. There are two
candles alight and many sacks. Isabelle, sitting cross-legged, is
swabbing his face with water from a basin. The Old Nomad is also
in the tent, listening.

HORSEMAN: We set fire to the village of Marguerite because
              farm by farm they had seized our land – the
              Roumis – and face by face they were spitting
              into our eyes. Nearly a hundred of my brothers
              were captured. I escaped.

The Horseman winces with pain and grasps Isabelle's arm.

ISABELLE: Do not try to talk.
HORSEMAN: We'll drive them out, force the Roumis back to
              their own drunk continent.
ISABELLE: Shhhh. Shh.
HORSEMAN: For those on the run, every pool is only as deep
              as the cat's paw is long. . .

He groans.

Isabelle lifts him up to make him more comfortable. His head
falls against her chest.

HORSEMAN: My body tells me you are a woman.

Isabelle bends down and kisses him passionately; he closes his eyes. She sits up.

ISABELLE: Madhourri!

The Horseman is dead.

SOUF DESERT NEAR NOMAD ENCAMPMENT – EARLY MORNING

Sand, sky, distance, all merging. There is an improvised grave. In it, the Horseman's corpse, wrapped in a winding sheet. The Old Nomad with his tentative blind man's fingers is opening the corpse's eyes.

OLD NOMAD: May he now see Heaven, and may the Angels come quickly to question him.

Isabelle, a prisoner between two armed Bedouin Guards, is being led towards the grave. They are holding her brutally. Around the encampment other newly arrived Bedouins with camels and horses.

BEDOUIN: The shit of those who eat with the jackals smells of them.

He prods Isabelle.

One Bedouin unslings his rifle.

Sidi Lachmi climbs the dune and comes towards them. He is wearing a turban of yellow and gold, a green burnous, and filigree riding boots.

BEDOUIN: We've brought you the informer, Sidi Lachmi.

The guard forces Isabelle to her knees.

SIDI LACHMI:	Who are you?
ISABELLE:	A traveller.
SIDI LACHMI:	Where are you from?
ISABELLE:	I came through Temmassine to Ferdjenn, through Ferdjenn to Moiet-el-Caid, through Moiet-el-Caid to Big Ourmes.

One of the guards pushes her head down.

SIDI LACHMI:	How did you warn the French about the raid on their caravan?
ISABELLE:	I didn't.
SIDI LACHMI:	Where are you hiding your fear?
ISABELLE:	I have none.

Sidi Lachmi makes a sign to the guards to release her.

SIDI LACHMI:	Which is your horse?
ISABELLE:	As it is written, if there were two horses, one to take me to happiness and the other to unhappiness, I would not choose, I would take the nearest.

Sidi Lachmi beckons to the guards to leave them.

SIDI LACHMI:	Where are you going now?
ISABELLE:	I want to study with you.
SIDI LACHMI:	What have you heard about the Qadrya?

Isabelle fingers her rosary.

ISABELLE:	I know your colour is green.

Sidi Lachmi turns his back abruptly.

ZAOUIA – VILLAGE OF QUEMAR – MORNING – WEEKS LATER

The Zaouia, adjoining the mosque, is the religious school of the local group of the Qadrya Brotherhood. Isabelle is kneeling so that her head can be shaved. The shaving finished, the man who is performing the ritual places a coronet on her head and a cloak over her shoulders.

The door to the courtyard is open and two men are watching the ceremony from outside.

> YOUNG MAN: The new Khouan is dressed like a man, rides a horse like a man, fires a gun like a man, and answers to a man's name. But the nape of his neck is a woman's.
>
> OLD MAN: When you're older, you'll know the difference between a man and a woman is brief.

PALM GROVE – EL OUED – EARLY AFTERNOON

Across the dunes it is difficult at this hour to distinguish between the white sand and the light. Date-palms grow around a man-made saucer-like hollow. On the north rim of this crater, where the slope down is steepest, stand a horse and rider.

The rider is Sliman, wearing a turban and gandoura. He is gazing at another horse and rider who have dismounted below, near a well amongst the palm trees. The distant figure is Isabelle. She is washing her body ritually, first the right side, then the left. She lies down near the well, eyes closed. Sliman climbs up a palm tree by the well. He gazes down at Isabelle. His voice speaks, but his lips do not move.

> SLIMAN: You are the hidden rose, the rose of all roses.

Isabelle smiles as if she has heard. Sliman, now standing over her, speaks with his mouth moving.

SLIMAN: The Captain sent me to Kouinine. I have to be
back in barracks before sundown. Why do you
say nothing? Do you want to make me ashamed?

Isabelle opens her eyes.

ISABELLE: Did you tie up your horse?

There is a small garden beside the well. In it grow carrots, mint,
little peppers, a kind of parsley. Very green. The whole garden is
scarcely larger than a bed, and it is irrigated by a network of tiny
ducts made by hand with plaster. Some of the ducts have been
dammed with coloured rags. The water is flowing slowly like
quicksilver.

PALM GROVE – EL OUED – EARLY EVENING

Sliman and Isabelle are lying naked, covered with her burnous.

SLIMAN: If the Captain hadn't sent me to Kouinine, I
wouldn't have met you.
ISABELLE: You would have met me anyway: it was arranged
before I was born, Sliman.
SLIMAN: Before birth, we belong to the world of the
angels, but you were well and truly born. You
are truly here on earth.
ISABELLE: How do you know that, Sliman?
SLIMAN: When I kiss your lips and your hands, you want
me to kiss your whole body.

OFFICE OF ARAB BUREAU – CONSTANTINE – AFTERNOON

Heavy furniture. New electric fan. A large, decorative aquarium of
mediterranean fish. Major Frioux at ease in a chair behind his
desk. Frioux has a promising career before him. Opposite him sits
Captain Junot, in his fifties, his unexceptional career almost over.

FRIOUX: I've read your report on the Eberhardt woman.

	Does she still live with the Spahi you mentioned?
JUNOT:	Yes. Sliman Ehnni, Quartermaster Sergeant 5th Battalion.
FRIOUX:	Can you add anything more?
JUNOT:	They live together in a ruin, and she pays ten francs a month for it. She has run up debts in the souk.
FRIOUX:	Does Sergeant Ehnni belong to the Qadrya?
JUNOT:	No.
FRIOUX:	Is there anything new concerning Eberhardt's relations with the troublemakers?
JUNOT:	All she wants is to sleep with the holy man.
FRIOUX:	Which one?
JUNOT:	Sidi Lachmi.
FRIOUX:	We have a file on him; we'll look at it.
JUNOT:	Don't be deceived by the men's clothes she wears, Major. She'd fuck anyone, Eberhardt. If she were a Kabyle, we could pack her off to a brothel. She'd get her fill of hot milk there!
FRIOUX:	Be careful not to have a one-track mind, Captain. The Bureau believes that the Eberhardt woman is up to something more dangerous than you seem to be aware of. We believe Eberhardt is a go-between for the Qadrya and the English.
JUNOT:	You'd have to be madder than the English to recruit her as an agent. She can't get enough Arabs into her bed, that's the long and short of it.
FRIOUX:	I want her kept under constant surveillance.

ROOM OF ISABELLE'S HOUSE – EL OUED

The house is on the edge of the town, next to the dunes. There is no furniture in the room. The floor is sand. Hanging on one of the irregular walls, Sliman's Spahi uniform. Isabelle, dressed as an Arab woman, is by the door which opens onto a sand courtyard. She is holding up two threads of cotton towards the feeble light. Sliman is reclining on the floor of the room.

ISABELLE:	How long the days of Ramadan are.

SLIMAN: The Crocodile has not eaten the sun, so the sun will go down and we'll feast all night.

ISABELLE: I can bear not drinking and not eating, what's hard is not smoking all day.

Sliman moves towards her, intending to embrace her.

SLIMAN: It's even harder not to make love.

Isabelle holds him at bay, showing him the two threads.

ISABELLE: Not until the sun sets, not until–

SLIMAN: Not until you cannot tell the difference anymore between a white thread and a black thread.

ISABELLE: Let's make the time pass quicker with a history lesson. Who were the first invaders of the Maghreb?

SLIMAN: The Phoenicians, the Romans, the Arabs . . .

Sliman begins to caress her ankles.

ISABELLE: No. After the Romans came the Vandals.

SLIMAN: The Vandals?

ISABELLE: How do you ever expect to get out of the army of the Roumis and find another job – if you refuse to learn?

He is caressing her knees.

SLIMAN: The sun is going down. It is going down now, now.

ISABELLE: After the Vandals came the Byzantines, and after the Byzantines the Arabs.

SLIMAN: Not the Turks?

ISABELLE: No, the Turks were later.

His hand is now between her thighs. Abruptly, in the very last light, he pulls up her skirt and buries his face in her lap.

SLIMAN: I can no longer tell the difference between a black thread and a . . .

189

MARKETPLACE IN GUEMAR – NOON – MONTHS LATER

It is very hot. An amateurish pencil drawing on the lined page of
a notebook. Next to a tethered horse, seated on a sack, Isabelle is
drawing what she can see in front of her across the open square
of dry earth. Behind Isabelle, seated on a camel saddle, a
Bedouin is sewing.

A French lieutenant on horseback rides past, followed by his
retinue. The Bedouin puts down his sewing. He assumes Isabelle
is a man.

> BEDOUIN: He can't sleep at night.
> ISABELLE: Prayer is better than sleep.
> BEDOUIN: I'm talking about the Haken, the Lieutenant.
> He only falls asleep, according to his servants,
> when day breaks. Where have you ridden from?
> ISABELLE: El Oued.
> BEDOUIN: Come. I'll show you something it would be a
> crime to draw.

The Bedouin leads Isabelle to a small yard where there is a line of
women, each woman holding a cock in her arms. A man with a
knife stands before an upturned wooden box. Each woman
reluctantly hands over the bird she has carried. The man slits its
throat and throws the carcass onto a pile of others.

> BEDOUIN: Last night, the Lieutenant couldn't sleep. So
> the Lieutenant has ordered every cock in the
> encampment to be slaughtered. Tomorrow
> he'll be able to sleep late.

INNER COURTYARD OF THE ZAOUIA IN GUEMAR – AFTERNOON

Several travellers are waiting to eat, men cooking on open fires.
Under the arches of the arcade sit three women veiled in blue.
One of these is Sidi Lachmi's wife.

> WIFE: We need more water! And do not forget the oil.

The fires are burning high. Isabelle in her role of Khonan accompanies Sidi Lachmi across the courtyard to a circle of small stone benches. They sit down next to each other on one of the benches and Sidi Lachmi places an open book on his student's knees.

ISABELLE: We were going to speak today, Sidi Lachmi, about fate.

Sidi Lachmi is searching through the book he put down. He does not reply.

ISABELLE: There is a question. Do those who fight, oppose fate? Can we rewrite the words of the future?

SIDI LACHMI: Our victories are written, our defeats too. But we were to talk of fidelity! Perhaps fidelity begins, also, with the word, the word given.

They are interrupted by the sound of approaching horses and Captain Junot, accompanied by two spahis, enters the courtyard. All eyes turn towards the officer. Sidi Lachmi is obliged to play the host. He stands and makes a stiff gesture.

JUNOT: Where but in the desert can souls who are drawn to each other meet so easily? I love these wide empty spaces, believe me. I envy you. I'd choose the dunes rather than a desk, if I could. I'd choose the dunes.

He sits down on one of the stone benches, takes off his kepi, and wipes the interior with a handkerchief.

JUNOT: I was passing by and wondered whether I could ask for a glass of water. I still have a long way to go.

Sidi Lachmi makes a sign to one of the servants who pours water from a pitcher into a glass.

JUNOT: You are preparing a celebration?

SIDI LACHMI: A simple meal for the travellers who have travelled far.

191

JUNOT:	I heard you had been away yourself.
SIDI LACHMI:	No.

The servant brings the glass of water; Junot takes it.

JUNOT:	To the south?
SIDI LACHMI:	I would need a special pass to go beyond Toggourt.
JUNOT:	A formality, sherif. But, of course, formalities count. You teachers of the Koran are the first to insist.
ISABELLE:	The formalities of your office, Captain, are addressed to your superiors at Constantine, not to Heaven.

Junot stretches himself and lifts the glass to his lips. Before he starts drinking, he freezes; he stares at a spot near him on the stone bench. A scorpion. He does not dare move or speak. Isabelle gets up and, with an experienced gesture, picks up the insect.

ISABELLE:	The scorpion is concerned about only one thing: to kill as many other beings as possible, because it knows that in the end it will kill itself.

She throws the scorpion into the fire. Junot quickly empties his glass, puts on his kepi, gets up, and leaves without saying a word.

COURTYARD – EL OUED – EVENING

A horse and a well. Isabelle has been washing clothes in an enamel basin by the well. On the sand she has arranged a white sheet on which she lays the washing to dry. A man's shirt spread out. She is putting her washed student frock beside it.

The door to the street suddenly opens. Sliman in his uniform as a spahi. As soon as he sees Isabelle, he slams the door behind him.

SLIMAN:	You were not here yesterday.
ISABELLE:	No, I was not here.

SLIMAN:	I was here.
ISABELLE:	You were here when you were finished at the barracks.
SLIMAN:	You didn't leave a word for me.
ISABELLE:	When I left I didn't know . . . I am yours, Zuizou.
SLIMAN:	You lie when you say you are mine.
ISABELLE:	No.
SLIMAN:	What do you do in the dunes out there?
ISABELLE:	I learn.
SLIMAN:	With the marabout.
ISABELLE:	Yes, and others.
SLIMAN:	I know what you learn. They lust after you, all of them, and you learn to please them.

Isabelle hurls herself at Sliman and starts to beat him with her fists. Not like an hysterical woman, but violently and effectively like a fighter. As she hits, she shouts.

ISABELLE: You learn nothing! You imagine nothing! You're weak! Why aren't you ashamed to be a soldier in the army of those who've stolen your country?

She tries to tear his tunic off him. He neither steps back nor resists. He stands there like a tree under the rain. Eventually this forces her to stop. She begins to cry.

SLIMAN: If I say something once, it is true for always. I keep my word and I want to keep you.

Very slowly she edges towards him.

ISABELLE: Sliman, my love, my Zuizou, O Sliman, my heart, forgive me, please forgive me. I will never hit you again, never, never, you believe me my Zuizou, never again. Say that you believe me, my dove, say that you forgive me, my master.

Silence.

ISABELLE: I will never hit you again and nothing can part us.

Silence.

OFFICE OF ARAB BUREAU – CONSTANTINE

Major Frioux is dictating to an old French military clerk. While dictating, he watches a red mullet swimming backwards and forwards in the aquarium.

> FRIOUX: To Captain Junot, El Oued. In reply to your report concerning Isabelle Eberhardt, alias Mahmoud Sandi, I hereby inform you that the Arab Bureau in Constantine is taking in hand all questions raised by her activity in the Military Territories. Henceforth all initiatives will come from us.

Frioux sprinkles seed into the aquarium for the fish to eat.

MERCHANT'S HOUSE – BEHIMA – A MORNING THE NEXT YEAR

The house is a rich one. Stone floor, wall hangings, silver trays. Six or seven men are sitting on cushions drinking tea in a large room with arches that give onto a courtyard, where there are tamarisk trees. Isabelle enters and sits down next to Sidi Lachmi.

The two are talking intimately. He whispers into her ear, rises to his feet and takes off his green burnous. She takes it and explains to their host, the Merchant.

> ISABELLE: Sidi Lachmi is going to pray. I hear you have some letters you'd like me to translate?
> MERCHANT: If you are willing . . .

Isabelle puts on the green burnous of Sidi Lachmi, lights a cigarette, strides into the yard, beckoning the merchant to follow. It is by now December and the weather is cold. They sit on a stone bench under an arcade; Isabelle pulls the cowl of Lachmi's burnous over her head. She gestures like a robed judge. The Merchant hands her a letter.

> ISABELLE: 'Paris, 18th December 1900. Dear Sir. . .'

194

A man with a beard enters from the village square. He approaches slowly, eyes to the ground, lost in thought. His name is Abdallah.

> ISABELLE: 'Of the 211 sheep shipped to Marseille on October 12th, 107 were found to be suffering from Malta fever . . .'

Abdallah ambles along the arcade, behind Isabelle and the Merchant.

> ISABELLE: 'Foreseeing that the meat of the said sheep could under no circumstances receive a selling certificate from the municipal abattoir, we were obliged to sell them on the hoof . . .'

Isabelle pulls the burnous around her shoulders. She is cold.

> ISABELLE: '. . . at a quarter of their price to unregistered butchers . . .'

At the end of the arcade a sabre hangs on the wall. Abdallah stares at it. Suddenly he tears it down and, with both arms raised, strikes Isabelle from behind. The sabre is deflected by a wire for drying clothes and hits her shoulder instead of her head. Isabelle falls forward onto her knees. Abdallah is seized by men rushing from every side.

Getting to her feet, Isabelle totters like a sleepwalker, to where the men hold Abdallah. Her gandoura is bloodstained.

> ISABELLE: What do you hold against me?
> ABDALLAH: I hold nothing against you, you have done nothing to me. I do not know you, but I must kill you.

A Young Man runs into the yard with a rifle.

> YOUNG MAN: Let me shoot the dog now!

Sidi Lachmi raises one hand in a gesture of interdiction.

SIDI LACHMI: They're waiting for us to kill him, so they can round up every Qadrya they can find.

The Young Man lowers his rifle.

ABDALLAH: God told me to do it.
SIDI LACHMI: Do you know she's a Moslem?
ABDALLAH: I know she – *she,* as you say – she is a Moslem. God wished me to kill her. God still wishes it.

Sidi Lachmi's Wife, who has been watching with the women of the household, comes forward.

WIFE: You're lying! God did not wish it – that's why she is alive. That's why you did not see the wire on which we hang our clothes. That's why the blade did not touch a hair of her head. God did not wish it. How much did they pay you?

Isabelle collapses.

ISABELLE'S ROOM, HOSPITAL – EL OUED – NIGHT

The windows are shuttered. Bars of light.

It is a military institution. Everything of standard issue. Two narrow metal beds, the second one empty. A shelf above Isabelle's bed, with a jug and tin mug. A small table with bottles.

Isabelle's left shoulder and arm were badly wounded. She suffers spasms of pain, her hand going rigid and clawlike.

The door to the passage swings open. In the doorframe, Dima. He is dressed as he was in Meyrin. He carries a blooming cactus which he places on the table.

He picks up Vava's revolver (it was not on the table a moment ago), and blows across its mouth. He strolls over to the wall facing the bed on which a handwritten page of regulations has been pinned.

DIMA:	'Sanitary Service Regulations . . . Disciplinary punishment which may be inflicted on civilian patients . . .'
	Can you be a civilian if you are as alone in the world as you are?
	As for Disciplinary Punishment, you have a fever of 40.2 centigrade. You have lost the use of your left arm. You are penniless.
	Your Sliman has tuberculosis.
	Have you found your garden?
ISABELLE:	Yes.
DIMA:	Do you want to know the end of your story?
ISABELLE:	Stay with me!
DIMA:	You didn't stay . . .

Dima turns down the blanket of the second bed, removes his shoes, lies down and pulls the bed clothes up to his chin. His head on the pillow is the face of a corpse. Isabelle is asleep.

ISABELLE:	The Cactophil is dead!

Gradually her face becomes calm. Sliman enters. The second bed is empty, there are neither flowers nor revolver on the table. He tiptoes to the bed, calls her name softly. She does not stir. He kisses her above the eyes, walks towards the door, has second thoughts and leaves a packet of cigarettes on the table. Tiptoes out.

ENTRANCE TO MILITARY HOSPITAL – EL OUED – MORNING

Sliman, sitting on the steps. The Military Hospital forms the fourth side of the quadrangle of the army barracks. A few eucalyptus trees. Captain Junot, accompanied by a French spahi sergeant, walks briskly by.

JUNOT:	Sergeant Ehnni!

Sliman gets to his feet, salutes.

JUNOT: You have no right to be here. The Hospital
         Building and its precincts are out of bounds to
         all other ranks unless in possession of a Medical
         Ordinance . . . You'd be better off, Sergeant,
         getting your kit together. You've been posted to
         Batna. A convoy is leaving at dawn tomorrow.
         You will accompany it.

Sliman falls forward in a dead faint. Captain Junot turns to his
sergeant.

JUNOT: Freshen him up with some water. And when he
         can take it in, tell him again he's leaving
         tomorrow at dawn.

The Sergeant throws water over Sliman's face.

QUADRANGLE OF MILITARY HOSPITAL – EL OUED – MONTHS LATER

Isabelle, dressed as a woman, arm in sling, is seated on a bench
under one of the eucalyptus trees. Beside her is Captain Junot.
Two soldiers are escorting a chained prisoner across the square.

JUNOT: The Doctor tells me his patient is doing well;
         soon, he says, she'll be able to ride again. I have
         a grey stallion that might tempt you.I share
         your love of fine horses.

Isabelle leans forward, her stick between her knees, to watch the
prisoner, who is her assailant, Abdallah.

JUNOT: He's being transferred to Constantine for the
            trial; he is unrepentant.
ISABELLE: However much I search my heart, I can find no
            hatred for him.
JUNOT: We could ride to Kouinine together, just the
            two of us. The horse is small for a stallion, but
            nimble, nimble . . .
ISABELLE: Still less can I find contempt for him.

She lights a cigarette without offering Junot one.

JUNOT: We are counting upon your testifying against
the accused. An example has to be set. These
Arabs are beginning to think they can get away
with anything.

Isabelle struggles to her feet.

JUNOT: Miss Eberhardt, I'm more than willing to put in
a good word for you, but . . .

She hobbles off with the aid of her stick, cigarette in mouth.

JUNOT: . . . my colleagues in Constantine are not likely
to forget how you are here with a Russian
passport. They can expel you at the drop of a
hat. Without any hope of return!

DOCKS – MARSEILLE – APRIL 1902

Early spring sunshine. Isabelle is among the passengers coming
through the Customs. She is wearing a burnous over her
shoulders, a wool cap on her head, and she is carrying a bundle.
The Welcoming Committee surround her. A lady offers a
bouquet. Isabelle is dumbfounded. A lawyer makes a formal
speech.

LAWYER: Miss Eberhardt. In the name of the Union for
Penal Reform we welcome you to Marseille,
while protesting most forcibly against your
banishment from the territory of Algeria. By
pleading for your assailant at his trial, you
showed a humanity that has enraged our
authorities. They expelled you because they
were ashamed!

Cries of 'Shame! Shame!' Clapping. Isabelle clutches the flowers.
The group walk from the pier head towards the street. The
Lawyer carries her bundle.

LADY: By expelling you they admitted defeat. It's a
victory!
JOURNALIST: Would you be willing to give an interview?

199

ISABELLE:	I can't help you.
LAWYER:	How did the accused react to your intervention?
ISABELLE:	With resignation.
JOURNALIST:	Do you think France will invade Morocco?
ISABELLE:	If it pays them.

A Literary Man takes Isabelle's arm and slows her down so that they are alone for a moment.

LITERARY MAN:	I'm the editor of a review published in Algiers – here's my card. I'll publish anything you write about Algeria, Tunisia, or Morocco.
ISABELLE:	I need money.
LITERARY MAN:	We will pay you.
LADY:	I read a wonderful story by you in the Revue Blanche.

The group arrive at the street and the tramway.

YOUNG LADY:	And you are not worried about the status of women in Islam?
ISABELLE:	You must excuse me, I'm late.
LADY:	We have arranged a little reception for you – it's only ten minutes away in a carriage.
ISABELLE:	I can't. I have an appointment here across the street.
YOUNG WOMAN:	Here?
ISABELLE:	Yes, with the King of Rats.

She takes her bundle and walks away, hunched up and limping.

AUGUSTIN'S KITCHEN – MARSEILLE – EVENING

The apartment is the same except that the seashells have been replaced by bicycle wheels and Hélène, the baby, is now four years old. The bicycle wheels hang from the ceiling near a workbench. Isabelle in her student frock, which looks too young for her, is feeding her niece at the table. Semolina and apricots.

HÉLÈNE:	I don't want any more. I want the story of the crocodile.
ISABELLE:	The crocodile who swallowed the sun?
HÉLÈNE:	Yes, the sun!

Isabelle arranges the contents of the plate to illustrate the story.

ISABELLE:	Here's the sun on a dune! Open your mouth. Once there was a crocodile who was so hungry he swallowed the sun. All the plants and animals were sad, sad. They couldn't live.
HÉLÈNE:	What did they do?
ISABELLE:	They died.
HÉLÈNE:	Like Grandpa?
ISABELLE:	Yes . . . like Vava.

Isabelle is for a moment lost.

HÉLÈNE:	Go on with the story.
ISABELLE:	Only the hedgehog didn't cry, because he was thinking.

Augustin comes in with a shopping basket. There is nothing left of the dandy. He sits down at the table and picks up Hélène's glass of water. He takes a bottle of pastis from his basket and pours some into the water. He raises his eyebrows at his sister. She shakes her head.

Hélène gets down from the table and tries to spin one of the suspended bicycle wheels.

AUGUSTIN:	Every humiliation we suffer is meticulously prepared.
ISABELLE:	Tiny, a happy life, like a classical play, needs unity of time and space.
AUGUSTIN:	Did you have time to look at the papers about the Villa Nuova?
ISABELLE:	No.

Augustin helps himself to another pastis.

AUGUSTIN:	It took me a month to believe. When the

	Cactophil removed himself from the business scene . . .
ISABELLE:	Don't talk like that, Tiny.
AUGUSTIN:	When Cactophil died, this scoundrel wrote to me. There's nothing left.
ISABELLE:	You're sure you didn't lose it all at cards?
HÉLÈNE:	What did the hedgehog think, Auntie?
ISABELLE:	The hedgehog was thinking how to get the sun out of the crocodile's belly.

Augustin leaves the table and spins a bicycle wheel.

AUGUSTIN:	That's how the Rostovski family has ended, without a sou, without a penny.
HÉLÈNE:	And hedgehog?
ISABELLE:	He pricked the crocodile so hard with his spikes that the sun fell out. Open your mouth.
AUGUSTIN:	Do you remember the garden and the summer house?
ISABELLE:	So the hedgehog said to all the animals: 'We must stand one on top of the other, high, high, high, 'til we can nail the sun back into the sky!'
HÉLÈNE:	I like the Hedgity Hog.

Augustin spins the wheel again.

AUGUSTIN:	Not a penny! We're dirt like everybody else.

Isabelle takes his hand and caresses it.

SHIP'S DINING ROOM

On the regular crossing from Marseille to Algiers. It is lunchtime and in the crowded First Class dining-room, Lyautey, now a general, and Eugène, now a major, are seated together. The Wine Waiter is attending to them.

LYAUTEY:	The Moselle, please waiter. We shall toast the coastline of Algeria. Ah, my Eugène, the sight

of that land brings back memories.
The beauty of the desert, the beauty of the
people . . .

The Wine Waiter pours a small amount of wine into Lyautey's glass.

LYAUTEY: Excellent.

The Waiter fills the glasses. Lyautey proposes a toast.

LYAUTEY: To the new country we are going to make. To our Morocco.
EUGÈNE: Our Morocco. Who says it is ours?
LYAUTEY: This is no time for modesty.

Eugène empties his glass, the Waiter refills it.

EUGÈNE: No time for modesty! Tonkin is a French provincial town stuck in Indo-China.
LYAUTEY: Are you still thinking, my dear, of your little nomad lover?
EUGÈNE: To the Eiffel Tower we will build in the Moroccan desert!

A Waiter brings food.

LYAUTEY: I admire your Isabelle, your reader of Pushkin and the Koran. She has become quite famous. Perhaps notorious is the better word.

Eugène does not touch his plate.

EUGÈNE: Who was behind the assassination?
LYAUTEY: In the archives and in the long hallways of the Quai d'Orsay, the rumour arose that she was a cunning and extremely dangerous element.
EUGÈNE: How stupid can they get?
LYAUTEY: Bureaucrats never appreciate the beauty of a soul that is true to itself. They considered her a rebel. And, of course, in their small minds they were right. But aren't we all rebels?

EUGÈNE: No, we are not.

LYAUTEY: Well, there are moments in love . . . and there
are moments in battle when we forget
ourselves. Like candles who burn themselves
out and bring light to the world.

Eugène drinks.

EUGÈNE: All we bring are little Eiffel Towers.

SMALL STREET – MARSEILLE – MONTHS LATER

Sliman and Isabelle arm in arm. Sliman, dressed in a suit, looks
unwell, with circles under his eyes.

ISABELLE: Five . . . ten . . . twenty . . . twenty-five francs!

SLIMAN: How much will it cost?

ISABELLE: I don't know. Augustin says it shouldn't cost
too much, particularly if we take them back the
same day, before they close.

They enter a small clothes shop.

CLOTHES HIRE SHOP

The name over the door is Baltounyan.

BALTOUNYAN: Dresses for a ball?

SLIMAN: For a wedding.

BALTOUNYAN: For the lady too?

SLIMAN: For both of us.

BALTOUNYAN: Here is the price list.

They study it together.

ISABELLE: Why don't we get married like we are?

SLIMAN: It's for the photograph!

ISABELLE: To put on a fucking mantelpiece!

Baltounyan brings out his ledger.

BALTOUNYAN: Names, please.

SLIMAN: Sliman Ehnni and Isabelle Eberhardt.

BALTOUNYAN: Eberhardt . . . Eberhardt . . . I've heard that name . . . Something . . . Ah . . . the trial in Constantine. Good God, we read about it every day in the papers. It was you?

Isabelle nods and takes Sliman's hand.

BALTOUNYAN: You behaved, if I may say so, Madame, like a true Christian. Unforgettable. Saintlike. There's no other word for it. Saintlike. Let me find you a dress.

Isabelle and Sliman wait. Baltounyan comes back holding up an extravagant white dress with a veil.

BALTOUNYAN: You must wear this one!

Sliman anxiously consults the price list. Baltouynyan makes a sign to indicate that money doesn't enter into the affair.

BALTOUNYAN: Isabelle Eberhardt! Try it on, over there. The honeymoon is where?

SLIMAN: For honeymoon we say: Seven Fig Days!

BALTOUNYAN: Are you going to stay in our country?

SLIMAN: When we are married we can return to Algeria. By marrying me, my wife becomes French, and with a French passport she can come back to my country.

Isabelle appears in the bridal dress.

SLIMAN: A flock of sheep would stop grazing to look at you!

BALTOUNYAN: It's my wedding present – but don't forget to bring it back tomorrow.

SHACK – OUTSKIRTS OF MARSEILLE

Isabelle, in her veil and wedding dress. Sliman in his suit. They
have walked several miles from the city, and are tired. A small
inlet where there is a broken wooden jetty and a wooden shack.
Isabelle pushes open the door. On the floorboards, a thin layer of
sand: on the sand, two mats. Some candles. Opposite the door, a
huge bunch of mimosa in a rusty bucket.

> ISABELLE: You like it? I spent days working on it. I had to
> walk a long way to find the sand.
> SLIMAN: Poor Zuiza!
> ISABELLE: No. I knew you were coming. I knew it before
> you wrote to me. I wanted this hut to be like
> our home in El Oued.

Isabelle finds a bottle of red wine behind her bundle and places
it on the sand in front of Sliman.

> ISABELLE: Bucket after bucket I fetched, but here the
> sand is dirty . . . Here the people are lost . . .
> how long it all takes, what we've been through!
> SLIMAN: You love your Sliman?
> ISABELLE: I love you all the time. Before, After, During.
> Shit! What does it mean?

Isabelle starts to undo her wedding dress.

> ISABELLE: The best joke of all is: You and I are now
> married! Before the Registrar in the Town Hall.
> Legal matrimony! What an end!
> SLIMAN: You didn't want us to be married?
> ISABELLE: You are stupid!
> SLIMAN: Stupid! Stupid! You never stop telling me I'm
> stupid. Why did you always want to go further
> with me if I'm so stupid?
> ISABELLE: It's so cold here . . . Maman is dead, Vava is
> dead. Cactophil is dead . . . he killed himself,
> you know that? He killed himself with gas . . .
> All the family was –

She makes a sign to indicate 'mad'.

SLIMAN:	Drink something!
ISABELLE:	You have four more fucking years in the army!
SLIMAN:	We can go back together now. They can't keep you out – we'll go to Batna together.
ISABELLE:	Batna! The word's like a prison. Worse than Bone!
SLIMAN:	We'll manage somehow.
ISABELLE:	Listen, I have an idea – I've had it before. Let's leave together.
SLIMAN:	Where?
ISABELLE:	We'll die together. To die together is the real wedding.
SLIMAN:	How?
ISABELLE:	Both of us together! We'll go.
SLIMAN:	Have you thought how?

Isabelle searches in her bundle and flourishes Vava's revolver.

ISABELLE:	It's our only inheritance.
SLIMAN:	Do you have any rounds, Zuiza?
ISABELLE:	We'll buy bullets tomorrow. And we'll leave together, the two of us.

Original line drawing by Isabelle Eberhardt

Act 3

MILITARY ENCAMPMENT – MOROCCAN FRONTIER – DUSK – 1904

A small abandoned village near Béni-Ounif, full of soldiers, camp-followers and animals because General Lyautey is assembling his troops in the region. A handful of ruins or never finished buildings – with walls, doorways, courtyards but no roofs – have become at night the improvised meeting place for soldiers, camel drivers and nomads.

Around a bonfire in the open, a number of black Sudanese musicians are heating their drums (to tighten the skin) in the flames. Men are lying on the ground, others sitting, some drinking mint tea. Rifles leaning against the walls. Everything is temporary, and yet an atmosphere of eternal waiting.

Some Legionnaires are sitting, not on the ground, but on boxes, a bottle of alcohol between their feet.

KARL:	The Dane was engaged to be married in Copenhagen.
ENGLISHMAN:	Instead, he's been buried in El Moungar.
ITALIAN:	Zero . . . zero . . . zero . . .
KARL:	To call the column to a halt there, you had to have a brain the size of a split pea!

A Swede is concentratedly taking his pulse.

ENGLISHMAN:	It was like announcing to those cut-throats: Come and do us!
ITALIAN:	Thirty-four who will sing no more.

Silence.

KARL:	You're taking your pulse?
SWEDE:	One hundred and twenty.
KARL:	Paludisme, my friend.
ENGLISHMAN:	What's that?
KARL:	Malaria.

The Sudanese start to play their drums. Music that seems to come out of the earth: the feet hear it before the ears. A number of

Mozkahzni begin to move with the music, but they are not yet
dancing. Three Old Women sit on the ground, backs to a wall.
Seated beside them, Isabelle, dressed as Mahmoud. A Camel
Driver bends down to one of the Old Women.

> CAMEL DRIVER: Ten years ago in Duveyrier, remember?
> OLD WOMAN: Liar! Nothing bad happened between us.
> CAMEL DRIVER: Bad! Of course not. There's nothing so good as
> that in the world, nothing so good.

Through the dust and the billowing robes of the men dancing, a
Mokhazni with a red burnous and black beard is staring at an
unveiled woman in the doorway. Very deliberately he passes his
hand over his beard, downward. The woman almost
imperceptibly shakes her head. An Old Woman leans towards
Isabelle.

> OLD WOMAN: Do you know what the hand on the beard like
> that says? It's a message and it says 'I'll let 'em
> shave off my beard, sign of my manhood, if I
> don't have the chance of lying with you
> tonight.' Do you miss him?

Isabelle nods her head.

> OLD WOMAN: The eyes of your beloved are two stars. On his
> chest are spring roses.

Isabelle plays with the sand between her fingers.

LANDSCAPE – BENI OUNIF – AFTERNOON

A desert landscape, very different from that of El Oued. It is
jagged instead of undulating. Isabelle and two children who lead
her by the hand are walking fast between the rocks. They show
her a grey camel lying in its death agony. From its grey eyes, tears.
(*Camels do weep.*) A Woman, unveiled, barefoot, rifle slung over
her shoulder, passes by.

> ISABELLE: In the name of God, the only God, do you have
> a bullet?

WOMAN: With the men gone and the dog bandits of
every colour everywhere, would –

Without finishing her sentence, she hands over the rifle. Isabelle
fires and dispatches the camel.

ISABELLE: Shall I tell you how it is? Adam says: 'I'm not
the father of the world, I've never seen
paradise. Lead me to God!'

MILITARY ENCAMPMENT

A Legionnaire is playing his accordion. One of the three old
women is in her usual place, with Isabelle seated beside her. On
the ground between them a plate of plain couscous.

OLD WOMAN: Last month, Fathima Zohra's lover was shot by
a *dijouch* and yet tonight, they say, she will
dance.
ISABELLE: Dancing to an absence is hard.
OLD WOMAN: My eyes can't see . . . your voice tells me you are
not well.
ISABELLE: Only fever. For days on end. Soon I'll go back
to my Sliman. He will look after me. It's been
too long. The eyes of my beloved are two stars.
On his chest are spring roses.

A voice shouts from beyond the ruins.

Isabelle strides to the archway that looks out onto the stones of
the plain. The Man who was shouting is on a small, galloping
white horse.

MAN: They have killed my brother! They have killed
my brother!

The horse is without bridle or saddle, and the rider is barefoot.
When the horse stops, the Man falls to the ground and rolls
there, as if in a fit, wringing his hands, and repeating that his
brother is dead. Isabelle crouches beside him, places one hand
on his back. The Man stops his contortions and sobs.

Isabelle walks away from him and the encampment. The
Legionnaire Karl addresses his Swedish friend.

> KARL: First of all he's a woman. Secondly, she's a
> writer. Thirdly, because she's a bit mad, the
> villagers here and the nomads believe she has
> baraka.
> SWEDE: Baraka?
> KARL: A touch of God.
> SWEDE: Have you seen her knocking back aguardiente?
> Jesus! She could drink me under the table.

Fathima Zohra begins to dance. A hundred men watch. Green
veil with silver strands, white bodice and violet velvet dress. On
the faces of the men, Arab and European, the same expression.
Not of desire, but of recollection.

> SWEDE: Look over there, by the archway. He's come
> back and he's watching Fathima dance.
> KARL: Who?
> SWEDE: Your one with the baraka.

QUARTERMASTER'S STORES – BATNA – EVENING

Sliman, in uniform but without a cap, is standing behind a
counter; it is the section of the stores that deals with uniforms.
On the door of a cupboard beside him is the framed wedding
photograph from Marseille. A line of soldiers waiting at the
counter. Each one presents a paper. Sliman stamps it with a
rubber stamp and then hands over the appropriate service issue.
A belt, a pair of boots, a tunic. The last soldier served, Sliman
locks up and leaves with a wrapped package under his arm.

CAFE NEAR BARRACKS – BATNA

The cafe is full of men, Arab and European. Sliman enters and
sits at his usual table, the wrapped package on his knees. The
other men, while drinking, are continually looking at a building
across the street. Its windows are shuttered, its double doors
closed and barred.

A trader approaches Sliman.

> TRADER: How many francs?
> SLIMAN: Fifty a pair.
> TRADER: You know where you are?
> SLIMAN: Batna.
> TRADER: I'll give you ten.

The Trader discreetly opens the paper of Sliman's package and looks inside at the boots.

> SLIMAN: Boots manufactured in France!
> TRADER: A friend got a pair of army issue for eight francs.
> SLIMAN: Not of this quality.

Two Spahis stop by the table. In the building opposite the shutters are being opened by a woman: it is the town brothel.

> FIRST SPAHI: You never come with us, Sergeant.
> SECOND SPAHI: Sergeant Ehnni is married.
> FIRST SPAHI: Is his wife at home?
> SECOND SPAHI: No she isn't. He can't keep her at home!

Sliman raises his arm, but controls his anger. The Spahis leave.

> TRADER: Twenty for the pair – take it or leave it.
> SLIMAN: One hundred francs more and I'll be able to join my wife. I'll give you three pairs for a hundred.
> TRADER: Four!

The barred doors of the brothel open, and men hurry out of the café to run across the street.

> SLIMAN: At this table tomorrow with cash?
> TRADER: Four pairs; one hundred. Agreed.

The Trader leaves. The Waiter comes to wipe the table. Three Military Policemen appear from behind the bar. Two seize

Sliman, the third opens the package. The Policemen handcuff Sliman and lead him off.

LANDSCAPE – BENI-OUNIF – MIDDAY

A small, irregular white building, shaped like a beehive. A low doorway without a door, no windows. Isabelle's horse tethered outside, head protected from the sun with a cloth.

Inside the building are two large wooden chests, as high as tables. These mark the graves where a marabout and his wife were buried, four generations ago.

Isabelle, who has lit two candles, is praying. Something surprises her. Hesitantly, she gets to her feet, teeters around one of the chests. On his back, an Old Man, eyes open and staring.

ISABELLE: What are you doing here?
OLD MAN: I'm dying.
ISABELLE: Perhaps your hour has not come.
OLD MAN: Once I was able to watch the sheep with my children's children. When I became too weak even for that, my sons carried me here, and it is here that the angels of death will come to fetch me.
ISABELLE: Which is your village?

The Old Man shuts his eyes. Isabelle leaves the tomb, mounts and rides away. Then, she slumps forward onto the neck of her horse.

FRENCH ARMY H.Q. – EARLY AFTERNOON

Many tents. A French sergeant has already noticed the odd behaviour of an approaching horseman and has sent out men to investigate. General Lyautey comes to the entrance of his luxurious marquee. Soldiers are leading the horse by its bridle. The rider is apparently unconscious in the saddle.

LYAUTEY: What have you got there?

A few steps and he recognizes Isabelle.

> LYAUTEY: Put him on my bed.

The Sergeant does not hide his surprise. Lyautey turns and walks back into his tent. Isabelle, supported under each arm, legs limp, raises her head for a moment.

> SERGEANT: Get on with it, you heard the General's order, place this wog on the General's bed!

MARQUEE OF GENERAL LYAUTEY

The large, high tent is furnished like a room, with carpets, cushions, a period dining-table with chairs, fine china, elaborate paraffin lamps. The predominant colour is deep red. The tent entrance is open and we see a Sentry on guard outside. Lyautey lights a cigarette from his 'eternal' flame. Isabelle is lying on the bed, covered with blankets. She stirs.

> LYAUTEY: How do you feel?
> ISABELLE: Done for.
> LYAUTEY: Getting better is a matter of willpower. You're going to get better, I haven't the slightest doubt. You have every reason to get better. The Arab Bureau is leaving you alone these days. You're free!
> ISABELLE: My husband is sick . . .
> LYAUTEY: So you really are married?
> ISABELLE: He's sick, he still has four more years to serve in the army, he's a Sergeant with the Spahi, Sliman Ehnni.

Lyautey turns to the Sentry.

> LYAUTEY: I want to know the whereabouts of Sergeant Sliman Ehnni.

He approaches the bed.

LYAUTEY:	Everything will be arranged. They thought I was at death's door six months ago, and look at me now.
ISABELLE:	You and I don't lead the same life.
LYAUTEY:	Come, come, a little less of your oriental fatalism. You have won the confidence of the Lords of the Desert. They listen to you and you will be able to persuade them that it is in their interest to go along with us. You and I are going to bring Peace and Order to this poor land.

He realizes she is asleep. Approaching the bed, he lightly strokes her forehead. As he stands there, a young Military Doctor arrives.

OUTSIDE MARQUEE

The Sentry salutes.

| SENTRY: | Sergeant Sliman Ehnni has been sentenced to six years of military prison in Batna. |
| LYAUTEY: | Order him to be released immediately. |

As the Sentry steps away, the Military Doctor comes out of the tent.

| DOCTOR: | A typical case of yellow fever. With good hospital treatment, the patient will recover. What I am much more anxious about is the patient's general condition. The patient has the physique of somebody thirty years older, due, I'd say, to every kind of excess. After all, she's a woman – |
| LYAUTEY: | Woman! She has the strength of three men! I want her sent to Ain Sefra tomorrow, with a special train and a nurse. See to it, Captain, and detail Major Eugène Letord to accompany her. |

DESERT TRAIN – NEXT DAY

A railway wagon, which has been converted for transporting the seriously wounded. Several beds, then a white partition with a door in the middle with a red cross on it. Isabelle lies on one of the beds, eyes shut. Eugène is sitting on the next bed, bending over her. The train goes slowly. The tracks are badly laid.

> ISABELLE: Stop the cocks crowing, Cactophil, stop them. Please . . . I can't sleep.

Eugène wipes her lips, changes the towel on her forehead.

> ISABELLE: The sun needs a nail . . .

A Nursing Sister comes through the door with a white box. She has difficulty in walking as the train sways.

> EUGÈNE: She is delirious, Nurse.
> NURSE: You insisted upon staying with her, Major.

Time passes. Isabelle opens her eyes and sees Eugène for the first time.

> ISABELLE: You!

She tries to sit up, and arrange her hair.

> EUGÈNE: Don't worry. It's only me.
> ISABELLE: Where are we?
> EUGÈNE: On the way to the hospital in Ain Sefra. Everything is all right. You'll be looked after. Your husband is coming.
> ISABELLE: When?
> EUGÈNE: In a few days.
> ISABELLE: When?
> EUGÈNE: In three or four days, for sure.
> ISABELLE: I don't want to go to a hospital. I'll get better more quickly with him, but not in a hospital. You know me, Eugene, I can't bear prisons.

EUGÈNE: Yes, that's something I do know.
ISABELLE: Thank you.
EUGÈNE: You're funny.
ISABELLE: Not always. Not always, my sweetheart. But tell
            me about you.
EUGÈNE: My mother died. I've inherited the family
            property. Vineyards, forests . . .
ISABELLE: So you're rich?
EUGÈNE: Do you need money?
ISABELLE: I did, but no more now. Tell me about you –
EUGÈNE: I don't believe in anything, Isabelle. I'll get out
            of the army and go home and busy myself with
            forestry and livestock and my tenants. In the
            evenings I'll read books and sit by the fire . . .
            and this will be my way of remaining faithful to
            you.
ISABELLE: There is so little to remain faithful to, look at
            me! Look at me, I'm a ruin.

One of Isabelle's feet is sticking out beyond the blanket. Eugène
holds her ankle as he arranges the blanket.

EUGÈNE: Do you remember the trouble we had finding a
            pair of shoes for you? Do you remember? It was
            in Bone. You remember Bone? I still want you,
            Isabelle, yes I still want you.
ISABELLE: It could be Death you want, my sweet one.
            Death can lure us all into bed.

She closes her eyes. Suddenly she tries to get up.

ISABELLE: Promise me, Eugène, promise me you won't
            take me to hospital. I want to wait for him in a
            house.

HOUSE IN AIN SEFRA

The town is on two levels: the upper town of military barracks, and
the lower town of small houses following the curve of a river bed.
Apart from a few stagnant pools, the river bed is dry.

A small house with a flat roof arranged as a terrace with a shelter of rushes. There is an outside staircase. In the street shops, goats and children.

Supported on either side by Eugène and the Nurse, Isabelle climbs the stairs to the roof terrace.

EUGÈNE: This is your house.

From the roof they look at the wadi and the few pools of water.

ISABELLE: And God divided the land from the waters – that's the first condition for a home, isn't it? Thank you, Eugène, thank you.

ROOM IN HOUSE – AIN SEFRA – A FEW DAYS LATER

A small white room with a beaten earth floor and a window giving onto the river bed. A table, some stools, a cupboard. On the table, some fruit. Isabelle's bed is a mattress on the floor. She is folding down the white sheets of the bed.

She straightens up, hesitates, goes to a cupboard, and then across to a mirror hanging beside the window. There, with great ceremony, she makes herself up. She paints her lips bright red. She is dressed in a white djellaba. She ties a white kerchief around her head. She blackens her eyebrows with khol. She looks out of the window and sees Sliman, walking down the riverbed towards the house. She cries out and hobbles towards the door, smiling.

ROOM IN HOUSE – AIN SEFRA – NIGHT

Isabelle and Sliman are lying on the white bed. Sliman pulls the kerchief off her head. Isabelle shuts her eyes. Sliman caresses her forehead.

ISABELLE: Take the things out of my bundle, Zuizou, we're home. At last we're home.

Sliman gets up, undoes her bundle and starts to put away her possessions.

He arranges a small pile of clothes on a shelf in the cupboard. He hangs up her 'student' dress on a nail in the wall. He puts her notebooks on another shelf in the cupboard. With the revolver, he hesitates for a moment, then places it on the table, near a half-eaten loaf of bread.

Lastly he takes out a handful of screwed-up envelopes and papers. From among the papers a drawing of a garden in a palm grove falls on the floor. He looks around and sees the bread, which gives him an idea. He chews a little of the dough, presses it between his fingers, and uses it as an adhesive to stick the drawing to the wall.

TERRACE OF HOUSE – AIN SEFRA – A FEW NIGHTS LATER

Moonlight. Stars. On the flat roof, Isabelle and Sliman are sleeping beneath sheep skins. Sliman's face is buried against her shoulder. Isabelle is looking at the night sky.

SLIMAN: You're thinking?
ISABELLE: Yes.
SLIMAN: What about?
ISABELLE: I'm thinking about our life. Perhaps it's because I was so close to death, within a hair's breadth, perhaps this is why I feel so much the pain of life and why I need it, this hurting life, like I need you, Zuizou.

TERRACE – AIN SEFRA – DAWN

On the roof of rushes heavy raindrops. Isabelle and Sliman are asleep in each other's arms. The noise of the rain awakens Sliman. He slips from under the sheepskins, puts a burnous over his shoulders and goes down the outside staircase to enter the room below.

ROOM IN HOUSE – AIN SEFRA – DAWN

Sliman is peeling an orange to take to Isabelle. The drawing stuck to the wall falls to the floor. He stares at it. There is the noise of rushing water. He goes to the door and sees a tidal flood advancing down the river bed.

RIVER BED – AIN SEFRA – DAWN

Sliman has been swept several hundred feet downstream. He manages to grab the branch of a tree and pull himself out of the water. At this moment he sees their house carried away.

> SLIMAN: Isabelle, I-sa-belle, *Iiii–saaa–belle* . . .

MARQUEE OF GENERAL LYAUTEY – NOVEMBER 1904

The General is standing by his table on which is laid out a large map of Algeria and Morocco. Near him stands Eugène. They are alone.

Lyautey walks down the tent towards the bed. Beside it, a lacquered trunk with painted dragons from Indo-China. On the lid of this trunk are papers and notebooks, many pages have been damaged by water and mud. Isabelle's revolver is on top of them.

> LYAUTEY: We found her under the ruins of the house. I gave the order to search everywhere for everything of hers that could be found. The search went on for two days and two nights, in shifts. One must always think of posterity, Eugène, always . . .